swim for the little one first

Other works by Noy Holland

What Begins with Bird

The Spectacle of the Body

swim for the little one first

noy holland

FC2

TUSCALOOSA

Copyright © 2012 by Noy Holland
The University of Alabama Press
Tuscaloosa, Alabama 35487-0380
All rights reserved
Manufactured in the United States of America

FC2 is an imprint of the University of Alabama Press

Book Design: Illinois State University's English Department's Publications
Unit; Director: Tara Reeser; Assistant Director: Steve Halle; Production
Assistant: Ameliah Tawlks
Cover Design: Lou Robinson
Typeface: Garamond

The paper on which this book is printed meets the minimum requirements
of American National Standard for Information Sciences—Permanence
of Paper for Printed Library Materials, ANSI Z39.48–1984

Library of Congress Cataloging-in-Publication Data
Holland, Noy, 1960–
Swim for the little one first / Noy Holland. — 1st ed.
    p. cm.
ISBN 978-1-57366-169-0 (pbk. : alk. paper)
I. Title.
PS3558.O3486S95 2012
813'.54—dc23
                                          2012013879

for Phoebe
&
for Benjamin

Be everyway alive.

"Swim for the Little One First" first appeared in *Conjunctions*; "Blood Country" in *Western Humanities Review*; "Pemmican" in the *Milan Review*; "The Last Doll Never Opens" in *Fairy Tale Review*; "Today Is an Early Out" in *Detroit: Stories*; "Jericho" in *Denver Quarterly*; "Love's Thousand Bees" in *Unsaid*; "Luckies Like Us" in *Columbia*; "Two Dot" in *NOON*; "Milk River" and "Pachysandra" in *New York Tyrant*.

contents

swim for the little one first

pachysandra

Rose called.

I said, "Hello, Rose."

"You sound funny."

I was lying on my back with my legs in the air trying to make a baby with my mister. I had his seed in there. My poor egg had slipped out to meet it.

"Can't you come out here and help me?" Rose pleaded. She had bunions. She had busted her elbow stirring oatmeal.

I was busy. My mucous was of a quality. I had just the least clutch of eggs left out of the millions I got when I started.

"Get off," my man said, "and I'll do it again."

"Is that Tonto I hear?"

Tonto snorted. "She'll talk all day if you let her."

"Just send me the obituaries," Rose said. "I want to see if I'm in them."

•

Come March, Rose called again. I wasn't doing anything. I was solo again.

"I broke my back," she said, "reaching for butter."

"For butter?" I said. "That's ridiculous."

"I bought you a ticket. I'll send Rudy."

Rudy was the help. He was wicked. His eyebrows made a lovely shade for his eyes. He was Hopi and his hair shone like butter.

I said I'd come. I flew across. Landed in the land of enchantment. I'd been a girl here. Been in quicksand in the big muddy river. I scrambled out.

No Rudy.

But who, after all, can blame Rudy after all we've done?

I caught a taxi and went straight to the hospital where I had come out into this world.

"Who was there," I asked, "anyone?"

"Gotcha. Big Ed and Snicker Bar were somewhere in the back."

Gotcha looked up weepily whenever Rose said his name. He worked to sit up and tipped over. Rose fed him off her fork at the table.

"I like butter," Rose told me. "Is it so much to ask?"

Her back was cracked in three places. She broke like pencils. She had a hump you could set your mug on.

The doctor said, "Doll, if you can get her to walk. Get her at least to sit and eat."

"Eat?" I asked him. "She will vomit in her plate."

I hated to so much as touch her.

Rose broke a finger dialing the telephone. She snapped the neck of her femur off stepping up the step from the driveway.

March and the jonquils were blooming. I had brought a few stalks to the hospital in a peanut butter jar. A bee buzzed in the cup. It made me sleepy.

"Are you sleeping?" I asked her.

"I will be."

•

I went home while Rose slept to scrub up the house. I'd find a nurse and sort through the cupboards—the blackened fruit and applesauce, the chewed-open boxes of Jell-O. Rose had cans from the 1940s. Sacks of sugar hard as adobe. She had a hip-high stack of aluminum pans the city delivered her meals to her in.

I'd move the bed. She needed a hospital bed, cranks and pulleys. The handsome doctor said so.

Under her bed I found droppings and newspaper, stuffing tugged from the mattress, insulation, sponge. I found the ossified stools of her dachshunds, still ruddy from Kips and Kibbles. The cretins snapped at me while I worked: Big Ed, Gotcha, Snicker. They pissed on my lumpy pillow. They ate every bristle of my toothbrush and threw it up in my shoes.

"You could take them to the vet," Rudy suggested, "and ask if they are in any pain."

"And if they are?" I asked.

•

I couldn't do it.

Rose had saved those dogs from the gas box. They had no manners. You couldn't blame them.

Gotcha had a tumor in his bowels. He puffed up and walked his belly raw on the carpet. Snicker was missing an eyeball. Something ate Big Ed's hair.

They chased mice and never caught them. Cockroaches feasted at their food bowls.

Candles went limp in their holders, helpless in the heat of the desert. Every doorknob was choked with elastics Rose had saved from the paper for years.

•

I rolled my sleeves to my elbows, afraid to have something run up them.

I slept blasted on the beach with Tonto one splendid week in Panama City. A ghost crab scooted up my pantleg. A fiddler crab sat in my eye socket.

"You made it up," Rose said, "but I like it."

The handsome doctor thought Rose was my mother.

"My mother is already dead," I told him. But then I wished I hadn't.

•

I wished I hadn't come. I wished I had Tonto to work with still, slow in a sunny bed. My time was passing.

Rose said, "Whose isn't?"

I held her sweet hand and looked out. A jogger streaked past the hospital window. He weaved between cars in the parking lot, sweating and showing off. He looked like Rudy.

He was Rudy. Rudy was supposed to be high on the Spanish tiles patching leaks with cut-in-half coffee cans. Half Rose's roof was cans. Rudy sprayed them a desert amber, glopped them in with a fat seam of caulk.

"Let me out," Rose pleaded, "before he knocks the house down."

She reached for the handsome doctor, her eyes sparkling in her head. She was jacked up. They call that comfortable.

That house was coming down around her ears. For forty years, the roof had leaked. The walls shed stucco like continents the English ivy had dug its fingers down in.

Everything Rose knew needed helping—Rudy and the gas-box dachshunds, the stricken DISCO elm. She knew a one-legged boy she took cookies. She married a man who was dying and spent her honeymoon in the hospital. A year later they were picking out coffins. The Big Pink. The Satin Amplitude.

·

"If you find me with my throat slit," Rose told me, "look for Rudy."

I looked for Rudy. Rudy was turning cartwheels in the street.

I was still inside cleaning. I cleaned up the oatmeal, the butter. Everything felt buttered. The soap grew mold, a green velour. The chairs wicked piss from the carpet.

I thought of Hanta, death by mouse, amazing what can kill you.

Rudy stayed away.

I bathed the dogs and they bit me. I set the organ to play *Moon River* and scrubbed my knuckles bloody.

•

The handsome doctor let Rose go. I got her squared away in her rented bed with the handcrank and the pulleys. Her house was clean but she didn't like it.

She liked yard sales. Topiary and porcelain, other people's pictures. She liked chubbies in bikinis and butterflies climbing the garden fence. Reminders, little helpful hints, tea tags and winged cookies: *Next time order the shrimp.*

She liked bacon fat and Jimmy Dean sausage.

She liked her bed I took apart.

"Rudy helped me," I lied.

Rose said, "Stonewall Jackson slept in that bed," she swung her feet until her slippers dropped off, "before he burned Atlanta."

•

Watch it, girl, those luscious mounds of ice cream topped with cherry
Can be the source of extra pounds that people note...just barely.

•

"I like your mouth," Rudy said. "I like your buttocks."

He brought his women to the pachysandra that grew beneath Rose's window. I watched them in the streetlight doing what people do.

I tried missing old Tonto but couldn't.

"There's something about you," I told Rudy.

"Maybe this?" he said, and showed me his package.

•

"Sow your wild oats on Saturday night, hope the crop fails on Sunday," Rose liked to say.

When there was moaning in the pachysandra, Rose said, "Open the blind and let's see."

Rudy waved at us. He was kneeling in leaves.

He was killing her with it, how it sounded.

Big Ed ran laps around the bed legs. His stool hung from the hole by a hair.

Something was leaking from Gotcha.

A pair of roaches chased Snicker from her food bowl until she was too spooked to eat. Rose fed her in bed, the TV blaring, her eyecup buzzing with flies.

Rose kept TVs on in every room of the house—half the day, all night. I woke to car chases, shoot-outs, Rose thrashing in her bed. We kept her jacked up. We lost track of the bones she was breaking.

We lost Gotcha, who had leaked for too long.

There was a big rusting freezer in the basement stuffed with meatloaf and frozen lettuce. City Meals for a dollar. Individual portions.

Rose had us put Gotcha in with them. He would keep.

"Throw the lot in there and bury me with them."

•

Rudy carried Gotcha down.

"Psst," Rose said. I can think of no other way to spell it. "Hopi eat dogs," she whispered. "They dance with chickens. They dress up like ravens and snakes."

Rudy carried Rose to her Naugahyde chair. He smelled like Gotcha. She fell out of it.

Rudy said, "You meant to."

Rose spat at him. "I'm starved. Give me a leg to gnaw on."

•

She quit eating. She didn't care if she lived. They gave her something for it.

We gave Rose a siren-flashlight for her to call us to her bed, to her chair. *Wao wao wao,* it went.

She motioned for me to bend near.

"Check on Gotcha," she said.

"Gotcha's dead," I said.

"Exactly."

He was there but an ear was missing. I turned him over to hide the deed.

•

I took to Rudy.

My next little egg went out. I picked life, was my way of thinking, despite the blah blah blah.

Rose said, "If at first you don't succeed, keep on sucking 'til you do suck seed."

Wao wao wao, the siren went, but we kept to the pachysandra, doing what people do.

Rudy had me knocked up come April.

Come April, Snicker died of poison. We found her in back in the sunshine, blown up and leaking foam.

"Get out," Rose said.

I had nowhere to go.

She said, "I'll tell you a cute little story."

She made Rudy sweep the flagstone where deer mice pissed and lived.

"There once was a little Indian," Rose began.

Drool crept from her mouth to her ear. She had hairs in her ears. I offered to pluck them. I plucked her whiskers. We drank Pabst from cans and watched the window where Rudy lay the pachysandra down.

•

No Rudy.

No Rudy in that house long enough it seemed he must be gone.

I took a photo of the last place I saw him—his buttered hair, his silken tongue. He took Gotcha, bundled up like a baby, already starting to thaw.

Rose said, "I never did have any babies. I never had brothers or sisters. My neighbors have been awful good to me. We make our choices," she said, and drifted to sleep, and waked and said, "and then we lie in them."

•

I lay in bed and felt the baby kick me, mine and Rudy's. Rudy was wicked. That didn't matter to me.

I couldn't say if the baby mattered to me or if it was just something that happened, like breaking the neck of your femur off on your way to driver's safety.

I caught myself in the mirror, pulled my face toward my ears. That was better. I didn't look long.

I touched myself and kept going. I went until the bees bunched up in my lungs, thinking, *Rudy, Rudy*—slow until they lit out through me, how lovely they used to do.

•

In the morning I went to the hospital and had them scrape what Rudy gave me out.

I would not have been much of a mother. I went for shitbags. I liked to sleep late. I liked people who could work their own spoon.

I stopped in for caustic green chili. It made my head sweat. It made me cry until I couldn't stop crying. I flirted with the waiter and stiffed him, getting back at Rudy.

•

Rose was singing when I walked in.

> *Won't you go on, Mule,*
> *don't you roll those eyes,*
> *you can change a fool*
> *but a doggone mule*
> *is a mule until he dies.*

I pried the window open. Something had shit in the grass. Maybe elephant.

The pachysandra was still matted down. I felt it for heat like a campfire the cowboys have ridden out from.

•

The telephone rang. It hadn't done that before.

"Is Spanky there? Hey, Spanky."

"Spanky?" I said. "Rudy?"

"Git back here, little bunny."

It wasn't Rudy. It was those characters down the street.

That night I tied a rag around Big Ed's jaw to stop him yapping when I went out. Even outside, I heard Rose sleeping.

It was just me and Rose and Big Ed now.

I walked to Spanky's. It was right down the street.

There were hookers outside in Barbie clothes. Strippers inside in sequins. They danced in cages. They lunged at the bars.

I ate French fries. I drank a nice cold Coke.

•

"You know I love you forever. But if you pour me a Coca-Cola I'll love you forevermore."

•

Pot roast, frozen lettuce, prunes.

Chicken leg, frozen lettuce, peaches.

Meatloaf, frozen lettuce, pudding.

Pot roast, frozen lettuce, prunes.

·

No Rudy.

"I could take you out."

"Only way I'm going out is in a coffin."

Rose quit singing. She ate a grape here and there if I skinned it.

She quit letting me pluck her chin hairs out or work at her ingrown toes. Her siren weakened. Her organ quit.

She quit sitting in the back with Big Ed. Come May, Big Ed was finished, dead of having lived.

·

I started in the far room pulling plugs on TV sets, the murders and the heartbreak, the vim and vigor of the news. The sound closed around Rose. She never noticed. I pulled the last prong and her room went *oooo*.

Now it was me and Rose and long desert days and three square meals she wouldn't touch anymore.

The siren gave out altogether and Rose had to call me by name. She forgot my name. She forgot I was there.

When she saw me, she said, "Who is it?"

I went to her attic and tried on dresses—much too short, far too wide.

"What do you want to do today, Rose?"

"Swing on the bars?" she said, her hands hooks beside her chin.

Her room filled up with butterflies. She was suffocating in them.

·

Rudy sent a photograph.

His chest was heaving from the dance he had danced. His face was shining, and the brave lovely wings of his back.

"We need air," I told Rose, "a little sunshine."

Every day was sunshine.

I suggested, "A little Tang party and tea."

I brought Lorna Doones to the front stoop where the rest of a world went by. The dying elm was spray-painted DISCO. A punk pinched a loaf in the grass. I thought I'd never seen it but I'd seen it a hundred times.

Rose struggled along behind her walker to the lip of the front stoop. I tossed her walker in the pachysandra. I hooked my arms behind her neck and knees and swung her softly up.

My bride, I thought, my balding doll. But everything in her was breaking.

"Oh," Rose moaned. And then, "Move it."

We lay on our backs breathing. The grass was pokey and dry beneath us. The leaves did their thing in the sun.

Rose held out her hand for a Lorna Doone. They were perfect. They were from the 1960s.

She would be dead before she got it to her mouth.

"Tell me something," I told Rose. "Tell me a cute little story."

"Fuck off," said Rose.

I was choked up. I ate slowly, my love, my last Lorna Doone, my old bloody country.

love's thousand bees

The boy was blind and from Zelienople. He came among us as a bear-child might, such a slumber, the sow labors in sleep, from sleep heaves up, raving and newly mothered.

The boy had fattened at the taps, sucked from the trees was how he reached us, wise to set out in spring. Our nights had warmed and the frogs thawed and, by day, sun weakened the trees. Sap twanged into our buckets. To improve these notes, the frogs gave up their two favorite notes from the pools.

The boy added to this the wheezing a fat boy does to breathe, and the slur, as he walked, of one pantleg against the slickened other. He slogged through the pools and his galoshes filled up. He felt with his hands for trees. We didn't know was he blind or did the meat of his face make it hard to see. We looked for his eyes, they were bloody, shot into his head from afar. We saw his scalp creased under his hatband, yeasty and flushed in the stubble.

The fields were too wet to plow; we had snow still patched about. So we busied ourselves in the sugarhouse, sweetening in the steam. We sharpened our hoes and shovels.

Spring, and everything wants to move. The children wake at daybreak and beg to throw from the mound.

The boy was spotted first beyond the backstop. Daisy, it was who saw him, lifting out of her trance on the swing. Daisy had clawed a ditch through the snowpatch for her feet to pass through to swing, who loves to swing, the one among us, the better yet to see. She sailed down in her skirts and went to him. She heard a kitten, who mewed in his pocket.

"Who are you and why are you here? Don't you have school like we do?"

He lived with Mr. U, he said, except that he said *yived*.

"He yived in #3 with me. I yiked how he was soft to me. Mr. U was yike some sock to me. But I did never yove him."

"So you want to come be here?"

"I guess."

"Geese! Geese!" Daisy cried out. Two flapped low overhead.

"Yovye," the boy said.

"What is the name of that kitten?"

"Goose."

"Goose?"

"Goose," the boy said. "You can have it."

"Does it fly in its sleep?"

"Maybe," the boy said.

"Do you pee in your sleep like my brother? One night he peed on my head."

"Mr. U peed in a bucket. It was my job to carry the bucket through the hanging-down fence to the stream. One time I dropped it. It went out of my hands in the stream. I had my kitten. I had my yittle chick in my pocket that died so I walked over here to you."

"Can I see?"

The boy held out the chick. It was muddied, a yellow wad of down.

"You can have it."

One of his fingers was off.

"Yook," he said, "I yost a tooth."

This he gave her also, a little milktooth brown as a scab.

He was happy to himself. His face was bursting. They heard the schoolbell sound.

"Wait," he said. "My name is Zach Syoat. I come from Zeyienople. My mother's name is Yenore. I have two sisters, Yenore and Yenore. I yive with Mr. U."

"Olly olly umpf," the teacher called.

Daisy waited still. The boy got out of his coat. He wore pajamas, slick and humid, a superhero's satin.

"Sweet," Daisy said, and pet him. The kitten smacked a fly from the air.

"I better go," Daisy said, and turned to go.

"Geese! Geese!"

The two came back.

"See you yater."

The door to the school bucked shut.

He had a tadpole, too, in his galoshes, he had caught, and a ball of goo, and a miniature shrimp, and to hold these, he made a bark-bucket for Daisy girl to find. The sap surged upward in the trees as he worked. His pajamas steamed from the heat he made. The jelly of his scalp melted open.

"Daisy mine," he breathed.

Love's thousand bees flocked to him, to draw the sugars from the heart, from the head.

two dot

I had a spot of luck and felt lucky. I stuffed my cupboards with Ramen—14 for a buck. That was lucky.

I had a job I liked beside the rodeo grounds. I liked the bar between me and whoever. I liked the regulars. A bullrider came in regular and left me great wads of twenties. The old skinnies came in, little birds, to sing. Among them Edith.

Some people make you feel lucky. I bragged, "I have a bird dog who sleeps through the night all night. A sky light in all three rooms. Three rooms. All the lonely little feelings of the planet are mine."

"Not a care in the world," said Edith.

Nobody gets off. This wasn't news to me. Not so easy. I had it coming.

I tied jingle bells to my boots in the woods—to spook away the moose, the bear. I stocked up. Pinched salt over my shoulder.

Should I leave my three rooms, I left my lights on. I hooked my radio up to a timer. I was there, all right. I would be back soon.

I worked nights, regular, the sun slipping down. I biked with the sun on my back. I rode the wrong way with my hair loose with my hair in my mouth and eyes. I rode fast. I saw it coming. I saw the guy never look, not a glimpse, gunning out. Here it was.

I was cooked. I had a foot in the clamp.

We slapped together—my tiny force against his.

My bike folded, neat. A wheel kinked and collapsed, teeth of wire, a snag. A scrap of my skirt flew among them.

You pick up where you go.

I picked glass from my neck. Black nubs of gravel buckled my rump—a negative sky with stars.

I stood up—I stood up!—and kissed him—the man who never looked. I was grateful and overcome. He took it nicely.

I'd have a clear patch now, accordingly. A bargain. I could walk.

I walked.

The road ran off up to Eureka, up to the sorry scraped-away slopes of the great blue felled Canuck timber.

They were waiting—my shrivelled, tender flock.

"Late again?" my boss said.

"Late again, boss."

He raised an eye at me. I tossed an olive at his teeth. "Stick it," I said.

I got my rag out.

"Not again?" he asked. "You swear it?"

I tossed another. I took a swipe at the bar, and poured. Schnapps, schnapps, pass it along, creme de menthe, little dove, Drambuie.

I pulled a red beer for a rancher. Dumped his cigarette butts in the bin. For this, he offered to break my arm.

Phoo.

I'd have a night of it. Pretty bullriding days. The sweet bulby asses of cowpokes ahead. The bar between us. He couldn't touch me. Phoo.

"Try to touch me," I said.

My boss was watching.

I pulled the beer first. Next juice. I sloped the glass.

The trick is do it slow enough the juice runs in a grubby tongue. Slow. I thought: summer. The coiled hose; the spigot on. The hose flumpy and hot in my hand. It's half a mile away—the first little glub and sputter. Hey!

Here it's coming, kid!

What a feeling—the old jiggle and dip. The hose wags up fat and happy, howdy, running hot and clean.

The juice pools if it's fresh and clouds. His did not.

His was making pulpy globlets. His globlets were rising, lacy and curdled, up through the yellow wash.

He threw it at me, our rancher.

You can't smell it. You taste it and it tastes like can.

He offered to break my other arm. He kicked a mother beaver in the parking lot, going out, going home, back to the ranch, there goes a man.

The ladies liked him. He never looked twice. He thought he didn't have to.

They liked his high thick wavy head of soap opera chestnut hair. His truck with heat, his acres. He was safety. The ladies fell for him from age, the poor twits, a dull dwindling desperation. Nobody looked at them: they'd disappeared.

I'd be disappearing, too.

I swiped at myself with my rag. I was wet. I tasted of can. My skirt clung to my rump. So what.

Pretty bullriding days. I poured, poured some more. I was in the clear. The big It girl. Deep in the Great I Am.

My girls tottered and twittered and drank, they were drunk. They were tired and weak and widowed. They went for creeps dead and living—the dead for they're easy to love.

They had stuffed their cupboards with Ramen like mine. Tomato soup in cans. They kept coins, bills. Figuring. Edith kept hers in the deep freeze, sorted and stacked in an ice cream box. Frozen assets. She'd be cleaned out. She spun on her stool and bragged.

I watched my bullrider try to work her. Easy. He was young yet. He could ride the worst bull to the buzzer and walk. He wasn't marked yet.

I told Edith about my radio, timed, my lights I left on, she said, "Oh?" She said, "I am eighty-six years old as of now. Ever one of these teeth is mine own."

Her teeth were green from all she'd been drinking. Her lips stuck to her teeth. She looked ridiculous. Her lips flushed the blue of her hair, mis-dyed. Her face was violet, satiny as a banner.

She was at suck, looked like. Her jaw was popping. She was draining.

He heeled back on his stool, our bullrider. He looked away to let Edith fall. She fell hard to the floor and twitched there, riding the bits and spatter of her busted glass.

He looked away—too late, too much. Some tough. Our bullrider went down, too. He passed out half upon her.

He took on the loose beauty of the fallen. His skin was polished—at rest perfected, his eyelashes heavy as a cow's. I knelt to kiss him. The others worked at Edith. It would be for me to revive him, mine to coddle him home.

She got her tongue down. A soft little gob of something cut loose and pushed through the slots of her brain.

"Do something," somebody said.

I took a swipe at myself. It wasn't me.

She was cooked. Poor poor. She had it coming.

My skirt stuck to my rump. He wore a buckle I liked. It was big enough to eat from. I said, "Edith."

It wasn't me.

Some days are better than others. Some people make you feel lucky. Edith was one of these.

luckies like us

On the ninth day, the mother put on her scrubs—not the clothes from home the father had laundered for her but the uniform of her doctordom, the get-up of a savior in starched and leafy green. He brought her the soft, loose clothes of the daily, clean, in a shopping bag she never looked in. She scarcely looked at him: she was a doctor, he saw she was occupied, she would look at him when she wanted. Speak to him, he knew, when she wanted. He was to stand until then at the foot of the bed with his hands folded over his zipper.

The skin had yellowed where the skull had broken and anywhere a tube, his daughter called them straws, anywhere a straw slipped in. He tapped the boy's foot, which was cold. He took the liberty of drawing the sheet across it, drew the sheet to the boy's blunt chin. The IV was backing and filling with blood and the boy had blood in his ears, did she know? Had anybody noticed that?

He turned away from her when he asked it, as though to check something beeping, a blip on the screen—he was grinning, a stupid hopeless grin, he knew, at how ugly she was when she bristled, the little doctor, the tendons flinching above the collar of her scrubs. Her face looked chapped and patchy. The vein that marked the middle of her forehead flared, dependably: she had heard him. He could read in her face what she thought of him. A man, just, a father. A donkey with a hammer and saw.

She went about her work pushing buttons, fussing with valves she rolled open and shut, nurse's work, filling in. He backed away from the boy to give her room to move and she moved between him and the bed. Her scrubs made the breezy important sound of somebody in a hurry. The boy whimpered. She let something of a mimicking whimper out, a mother sound he had heard her make in all the days before.

The news was worse on the ninth day. On the seventh, they unwound and patched the boy's bowels and stuffed them back in again. On the ninth, his brain was bleeding.

The mother pulled the sheet to his chin again.

In a moment she would turn, ask the question. This was not the father's domain but he could read it: the etiquette of the bedside, the arithmetic of delay. Let him wait. Let the loved one prepare to be grateful.

He didn't wait well. He lived by motion—plank and nail, joints cleanly held—rough work, not finish, a wall going up, work you could see you had done.

She was right: he did not even know the right questions. The building made him weary and sick to be in, the abandoned wings, the weird quiet. The smug, clubby ways of doctors made him sick, and how she tipped her head like a bird. (Now she would ask it.) "What was your—?" (He would slug her if she asked it.) "What was your question again?"

"I said—" and he asked her again. He saw her start up the little assessment that would tell her what to do, whether to answer or not, check the boy's ears or not, and he counted time on his fingers. It was a doctor's assessment, and a wife's, a guess, and he knew it was half concluded. It was swift.

He went through the questions: Had he been—in the past—grateful?

Was he ready to be grateful again?

•

The father kept away when she put on her scrubs—for days at a time, in the house he had built. He kept away with their daughter, playing checkers, eating cheese, sliding on the lids of dog food cans down the hillside in their helmets. He dressed his daughter in flowers and plaids, in dots and the splotched animal pants in vogue with the young that season. She wore cheetah pants in purple, cheetah hat and mittens, her hat pulled down over her eyes.

They stayed up late eating popcorn and they slept in their clothes in the mother's bed where the girl had been, far from the hospital, almost suddenly born. She asked her father to tell her the story.

"One thing. Tell about your sock I wore for a hat when that stuff was all over, right, that waxy stuff that was bloody was smeared all over my head? And Papa you drove," she said, "and Mama was just quiet. And Henry wasn't there, right? Henry wasn't born."

She stuffed her mouth with popcorn. She said, "I was in the accident, too, you know."

Popcorn shot out of her mouth as she talked. The father held up his hands in front of his face as though to shield it.

"Don't," said the daughter, and hit him, and she hit him again and again.

•

The daughter said, "One thing."

She said, "Let's never go back to that hospital where they use all those whistly carts and stuff and Mama is just sort of *wah dee ga* and she just never listens? Remember she forgets? Remember that time she said that to me? She said she would fix my hair."

She said, "I want to stay home with my pictures."

The girl was cutting out pictures of flowers and of women in bikinis from catalogs. She couldn't wear any bikinis. That was not nice for girls. She pasted the pictures on a page together and x'd out all the girls.

Her mother hadn't picked her. That was what the daughter told her dolls. Her mother had longer to love her. She had been alive a longer time than Henry and also she was a girl. She was a little mother.

The daughter had a cut lip that was healing and both of her knees were not bony or loose the way they used to be. They were puffy and hurt if she walked much but that was not going to make her—they weren't dashing *her* down to that hospital to fix her up again.

She carried her dolls in her underpants—two dolls tucked in at a time in turn so they would not be lonesome and they were all girls. If her babies were ready to plop out, *then* she would go to the hospital, but they were in her growing still and they were all girls. All God's little children.

She said, "Maybe you will die. Maybe God will want you."

She could not help it. All God's little children. She would say so long, goodbye.

·

The daughter told her teacher, "Henry's on vacation."

It was what she had said of her father, too, "He is taking a vacation from living with us still."

Still they had their days together—the ninth, the tenth, a few of the days that came after. The father closed up his house on the windswept farm on the curve of the road his children passed with their mother on the way from home, from school.

It came again to be the father's job to ferry his daughter to school. He watched his daughter's face in the mirror as he drove. She looked sleepy, and puddled in the seat, blinking.

She said, "You should watch the road."

She brought her dolls with her in a clump by the hair, lassoed at the waist with a bolo tie.

"There you go," she said, and buckled them in.

And: "Amn't I a so-good mother to you? I am buckling you right, right in."

·

He took his daughter to school and back again and drank in the sun in the afternoon in the house he had been let to live in with them. He sat in the window with the sun on his face and listened for the coughing and spitting of the spigot that would mean the pipes had thawed.

There had been a day of rain and thaw. Now everything had frozen. The birches had lain down their heads in the snow and now the snow had seized them—the snow had them. The birches jerked in the wind. He found it funny, and called his wife. She was his wife still. The trees looked frantic.

He said, "They look like a bunch of old women out there frozen in by their hair."

He said, "I went ahead and built that bunk bed for them with the boards I measured and saved. I took the Christmas tree down. The pipes are frozen. Everything is frozen. I rolled the tree into the creek bed. Lucy bled all into the snow. She got a nosebleed—she was sledding—she bled all into the snow. God, the snow. It's been blowing. It's scoured. It's blazing out there. I can't see."

The house grew darker. The windowpanes rattled in their tracks in the wind and wind drove the snow in between the panes into miniature drifts on the sill. The drifts darkened the house. The sun burned on the snow. The snow had a glaze poured across it that even the ox the neighbors kept did not, as it walked, break through.

The mother said, "He doesn't know me. He hasn't the faintest idea I am here."

•

The mother slept in a chair beside the boy's bed and waked when anyone came in. She talked very quietly to him, not knowing if he could hear.

"When I was little," she said, "by accident, my mother set fire to my hair."

"A bird snatched a sandwich from me."

"My mother weaved a crown of flowers for me and I ran through the garden naked, painted up, making soups of sand and leaves."

She said, "Wake up. Wake up, Henny. Mama's right here."

The boy had a hose down his throat to breathe and he held it, the way a baby will, the way a boy holds the branch of a tree he has climbed and is swinging through the shadows from.

•

The girl fell on her back from the monkey bars from swinging in her mittens.

Her father came early to fetch her. He came at Thank You Time. She was thanking each one of her dolls. She thanked the nurse for her Band-Aid. She was wearing a Band-Aid stuck to her head where her brother's head was broken. She thanked her papa. He was a good papa. She said, "I always buckle my dolls."

"He makes me popcorn," she said. "I would like to thank him. Papa, thank you, Papa, for giving me this—what's it called again? This bolo."

She was swinging her dolls by the hair.

They had a Thank You Rock they passed, each to each. The teacher held out her hand for the rock.

"I amn't finished," the girl said. "He made a ladder for me. I like these brown spots on his hands. He smells like bread to me. Thank you, Papa. Thank you for making me popcorn. Thank you for ice in my water. Okay, next now."

She passed the rock. "Say you're welcome."

He could not say much: he had lost her. He would lose her again and again.

•

To her mother, she said, on the telephone, "You could have gone into the snow, couldn't you? It would not have killed you. You could have buckled us all all in."

The police, too, had questions they called with. The woman from the insurance called to say, "Lady, your son can sue."

The mother said, "My son is two. His favorite color is blue, or it was. He liked to play blocks. He made a good sound like a siren. He's just small and he's sleeping and he will wake to himself and say *blanket mama me*. And you? You can't be—are you serious? You can't be serious. You are calling me and telling me, lady, he can sue?"

"When he's older, ma'am."

"So sue me. Put me in jail and sue him. I was in my lane and here he came and there was nowhere for me to go. It was morning. We were driving up the hill in the snow. It went shadow and sun and shadow and do you know what I was thinking? I was thinking, 8 or 9? I was going to buy skates for my daughter and I couldn't think 8 or 9, what the size was, I knew the color. Sun. And shadow and here he was. I thought I was seeing something. I waited for him to correct himself. I saw nowhere to go. The guy was driving a car like their father's and I thought if he was their father but it was not him. He was a guy from around. I patched him up once. I cut a rusty hook from his eyebrow once."

•

The twelfth day passed and another. Nothing felt right—not going, not staying away. He hated to call but he called her. Did she need the clothes he had laundered for her or the pot pie he had made or the bread?

"You made bread?"

"Well, I tried," said the father. Which he hadn't.

It amazed her—that anyone still made bread. That anyone tended lightly, easily, to the household, the press of tiny cycles, children's simple needs. *Blanket. Mama. Hungry. Pee.*

How many times had she wanted to run out screaming from him?

Dirty, ornery, noisy boy.

And now what would she—just to dress him, for a kick in the shin, to wipe his backside—what would she not give?

She rubbed his belly—hot, distended. He used to say, days ago, used to, "I want to feel your hot skin."

He was a boy who once lay so quiet in the grass a honey bee stood on his nose. The neighbor dog pissed on his bottom. She thought of him standing in a backyard pool hoisting an enormous zucchini. Of the ocean, she thought, the first time he saw it. A wave came over her head.

"I tried to run from it," his mother told him. "It was breaking. I was holding you over my head."

•

The daughter called to speak to her, to sing to her, something made up, come suppertime, a song of ice and trees. But her mother wasn't answering. Her mother had stopped answering the phone.

The girl spoke into the dead receiver. She bumped her nose against the counter to get it bleeding as she spoke.

"Papa's cooking," she reported. "He's a yogurt." (It was her brother's word for ogre.) "Now he's not. He's being that cooker that's fancy—right?—with the clogged-up nose. I got a nosebleed," she said. She tried to hide it. "And a fox came and ate up the melty stuff where I bled all down in the snow where the snow—"

"Papa, don't," she said. "I'm talking. Please don't turn that on."

The snow looked like a cherry slushie. In the morning it looked like a hole in the snow that a fox had come to see.

She said, "Mama, my tooth is looser."

And: "My papa fixed my hair."

She said, "I love everything you are cooking."

She liked him cooking. She liked the spots on the backs of his hands. She liked how if ever he took off his boots, he stood them back up again. They smelled of sawdust. There was sawdust packed into the treads.

She cleaned his boots for him, and shook talcum into the toes. She had an accident—and scorched his shirt with an iron.

They were like other days, these days, how they passed—her mother at the ER, her papa steady, home.

But they would be finished come morning.

In the morning, she would pour out cereal for her father and pick the caught bits from his beard. She would find his calculator—

his *cowcutator*—and take that. She'd take a rock to pass, a ball and jacks, a quiet pull-back train. Only quiet toys. Her father told her. You had to keep very so quiet there. You keep quiet when your brain is bleeding. You keep yourself so, so still.

She bent her nose some, and drummed at it with her knuckles.

She found her brother's best sit-and-ride toy and rolled it out into the cold. The trees creaked and popped. She liked the sound of them.

She shoved the toy down the stairs to take. The ox fell down in the field. The girl mooed to him. Her papa mooed back.

They would see Henry Bear in the morning, unless the ice came, unless the snow.

•

The mother settled into her chair as if to sleep.

He had brought fresh panties for her, and the line emblazoned on them kept repeating in her head. *More whiskey.* (A joke from the old days, a busty, puckish cowgirl, a lariat overhead.) *More whiskey and fresh horses for my men.*

The news was the same and the same and worse.

She drew her knees in, shut her eyes. Again the phone started up. They were after her: she was somebody else's mother. She was still somebody's wife.

The doctors appeared, went off, clammed up. Stingy bastards— pretending to hurry. Getting out, out the door, down the hall, man—quick, before she cries.

She should lock the door, yank the phone out. Doctor him herself.

She worked the ER. She'd seen plenty. Things they never had seen, she had seen—manglings, flayings, freakish stuff, the slop and stink that didn't make the cut for prime-time TV.

She had the head for it: the body gone at. The fat man disemboweled.

She had her face along the highway on a billboard.

•

She put clean scrubs on. Her boy whimpered. He shut his hand, opened it again. When he opened his hand, the phone rang again.

"Officer Sweet here." You bet. "One question."

She lifted the receiver, dropped it back onto the cradle again. Seconds passed, a minute, and up it started.

Her boy's hand opened when the phone rang, opened again, as though the ringing were a sound his body made and emitted through his fingertips. It sounded howly, living. The room was darkly purpled. She watched his hand move—a howling, pulsing flower, she thought, a bud caught in time-lapse footage, passing through the seasons, through the years.

He was two. He had not even learned to run quite. He still threw sticks backwards.

She tried not to hear the phone. It seemed louder then. She tried to quiet it by listening.

Her boy thrashed in his sleep. She shook him lightly. He hissed at her when she shook him. Blood bubbled out of his ears.

•

The father said, "Up, up. Time to scoot."

The girl brought sticks for her brother she had dug from under the snow. She brought dolls and the dresses she had made for her dolls. She made a long gown of raw bacon she poked twigs through the fat of to hold.

She told her dolls, "Sometimes when your nose bleeds. Sometimes when your brain bleeds, you have to just swallow it down."

She rode in back behind her father with her family of dolls. Her father rolled up the window on an out-folded map so the daughter's eyes wouldn't and her doll's eyes wouldn't sting in the so-bright sun. When he got the map right, he kissed her. She said, "Kiss Mama, too," and held up the doll who was the mama who was wearing the bacon gown.

The daughter's cheeks were shiny with grease and she was wearing a lacy pajama top and her hair had not been combed. He bent to kiss her again, her head tipped back, her narrow face turned up to him, a miniature of her mother's, and the daughter thrust her doll at him, saying, "Mama's right here."

"Cousin?" she said, addressing her doll. "Listen to me, cousin. I can show you. There's a thing with just marbles and springs we can see, and ditches with pops and whistles. This ladder thing carries this ball up. Okay? That is not for sick kids. That is for luckies like us."

•

It was easy for her to walk but he carried her and, as he carried her into the hospital, she sang.

This pretty planet, she sang,
spinning through space.
My garden, my harbor,
my holy place.

•

And then:

Bis bitty banet
binning boo bace.
By barben, by barbor
by boly blace.

•

The halls smelled of macaroni. She said, "I'm hungry, Papa. I want to eat, Papa."

He kept walking. She picked something out of his beard, tossed it in her mouth.

"Better now?"

"No," she said. "No way, I'm not. No."

She felt like eggs, or candy. She felt like having a snowball fight.

"You're so stupid," she said. "She won't like it."

She said, "You should have fixed my hair."

The father found the room, the door pulled to. He swung it open, stood without walking in.

The bed was tucked and smoothed. The boy was laid out naked in his mother's arms—living, he didn't know, or dead. The father held on to the girl.

She said, "You're hurting me, Papa. Papa, stop."

Still he held her, awaiting the news of the day, the life ahead, unstoppable. His daughter slid down his chest and off and he felt he might float up. He minded himself, meant to steady himself, make bone of the sand his bones became, put a stop to it. He was pouring into himself. Sinew and gristle, the renewable heart, the hard little beans of his kidneys—everything in him was mixing, slop, a caustic, grainy wash. He stiffened his skin to keep standing.

His wife waved at him. It rose up in her: the swarmy, passing happiness of seeing him again. She could smell him, it made her giddy: a man come in from the cold. *More whiskey,* she thought, and wished he would kiss her. Cross the room and kiss her. Fall on his knees and forgive her. For an instant, all at once, how hard could it be? She could ask him to forgive her.

He stood away from her, his hands folded over his zipper.

The daughter's doll began a dance, dancing gently, wildly, the bacon smacking against her legs. When she had finished, the doll fell on her back and glistened in the sun. In a whisper, the girl asked, in her doll's voice asked, "Do you think that dance was so pretty?"

"Oh, yes," her mother said.

"Not you," the girl scolded. "I asked Henry."

The sister reached in among the loops and straws and patted her brother gingerly, leaving little slicks of bacon grease. She pulled toys out to give him from the sack she had brought, saying, "Brother, I brought you this one, Brother, and that and that and that."

"The ox fell down in the field," she said. "I was swinging in my mittens."

She poked him gently. "You're not listening to me, Brother. He can't hear."

She blew into his ear and the hair lifted up.

He wasn't Henry yet. She wasn't any Henry's sister. She was a mother-girl with a bacon-doll with no little man to love.

"Hen, Hen, Hen," she said.

She kissed his head where he was hurt and stood up. She found the pull-back train in the sack she had brought and pulled it back across the floor to release it, to catch it up again. She would take it back home, she decided. The rest of the toys, he could have when he waked, finding that she had been near.

The daughter tugged at her father's knuckle to make him kneel for her, and spoke in a whisper to him.

"We can go now," she said. "He's just quiet. Little Henny's just being quiet in the dream of his life again."

jericho

The room was hot and dark and the children were sitting eating with their hands. The air smelled of rice and diapers. The children sat in chairs made for children or kneeled on the dirt floor. The floor was freshly swept and the lines the broom left in the loosened dirt still showed.

Rice fell from the children's mouths as they ate. The old señora who cared for the children would sweep out the room when they had eaten again. She would put the collar on the blind boy again who had pulled it off and dropped it.

He was always pulling his collar off and dropping it and he fought her when she cinched the collar back on but he swung his head loosely without it as though he had no bones in his neck. He had a skinny neck and the bones showed. His skin was the brown of an egg. If she let him swing his head, he would begin to dance and soon the dance became wild and fast and took up the whole room. The dance frightened the other children. So the señora would have to fight him.

She was old and she didn't like to fight but the younger women had jobs in the town and the mother who was the blind boy's mother had gone off to Guayaquil. She was fifteen and nobody blamed her. The boy had been blinded inside the mother by the medicine that saved her life. Nobody blamed her. She would have a life now. She danced at night in the discotheques and had her eyebrows tattooed on.

The señora sat in her chair made for children and watched rice fall from the children's mouths. She was as big as a boy of ten. She wound a sash about her braid to keep tidy.

·

She had been a girl once with her father in the city of Guayaquil. Her father bought sandals for her in Guayaquil with tiny beads and sequins and, when she returned to the town, all the other girls were jealous of her for a time. The beads were the eyes of flowers, luminous and blue.

Some things should be beautiful.

The bowls the children ate from were beautiful. At the bottom of each bowl, the señora had painted a fruit that grew in their yards or on trees near the town—*chirimoya* and *maracuyá, guava* and *tomate de arbol.*

She painted the face of the mother on the bottom of the bowl the blind boy ate his rice from. Of course he would never see it. Even if he waked and could see by some accident, he would not know it was the face of his mother who had gone off to Guayaquil.

·

"*Mami*," said the boy, and held his bowl out to say that he was hungry.

The señora kept very still in her chair and watched the other children watch her. If she moved, the boy would know where she was. He would stand on her feet and twist her skirt in his hands and say *mami*.

The other children liked to play at being blind and swung their eyes up so the color didn't show and bumped into things and stumbled. The blind boy only stumbled when he danced. His eyes were the luminous blue of the beads of the sandals the señora's father had given her as a girl in Guayaquil.

She held herself very still. She had one *dulce* in her pocket.

The blind boy came at her, as she knew he would. She had his collar in her hands. The collar was foam and dirty. She caught him under the chin with it and when he went to his knees as he always did, she cinched it at the back of his neck.

The boy clawed at the collar. He rocked from one foot to the other. The señora said something soothing and the boy made a sound that was not a word but a sound like a cat or a monkey. He pulled the collar off and his head swung free and he began his little dance with his bowl held out.

"*¿Qué haces?*" the señora asked him.

There was no more food and he knew it. There was never more food after the first bowl and the children knew not to ask.

The blind boy's dance grew wilder. He slapped his arms against his sides. His head swiveled on his neck. He rocked from one foot to the other and spun until he stumbled. He fell against the girl who was the smallest girl and she struck him hard and cried.

The blind boy went on dancing. He was always happy, dancing. He danced until he could hardly stand and when he stopped he wore his beautiful bowl like a hat and stood with his legs far apart so he could stand and the dark shapes swam in his eyes. The dark shapes were all in the world he could see and he only saw them when he was dizzy from dancing.

The señora let him be. He would be happy for a time. She would not have to fight to put the collar on him and he would go in his collar to the corner where he slept and the señora would have her chance then to sweep the rice from the floor. She swept the rice out the door into the terrible sun where the children jumped rope and ran.

·

He slept without moving, her little *ciego*. He made his long sounds like a mule.

She had one *dulce* in her pocket. She knew by the shape and smell of it what flavor it would be.

When she had washed the bowls and stacked them and wiped down the chairs and swept out the rice, she took the *dulce* from her pocket and gave thanks for it. She gave thanks for the children and for the fruit in the trees and thanks for her good broom, too.

She unwrapped the *dulce* and the blind boy waked. She said his name and he came to her.

Jericho stroked the tops of her feet with his feet. He smelled the *dulce* in her mouth.

He would be patient; he knew to be patient. He heard her tug the sweetness from it.

Jericho found the señora's face with his hands and drew her mouth to his mouth and waited.

He mustn't whimper, he knew. He mustn't ever brag or move his feet to dance or tug at the señora's clothes. Jericho mustn't blame his mother.

His mother was beautiful, they all said so. She had her eyebrows tattooed on.

The señora pushed the *dulce* to the tip of her tongue and she let him with his teeth pull it onto his tongue. Only Jericho she let do it. Jericho was such a good boy is why.

blood country

The wind came down from the mountains and drove the fire across the plains. The fire burned fast and bright now and everything living moved with it, the jackrabbit and the antelope, the coyotes flushed from their dens. The badgers dug in. He tried to think of it. He thought of his wife but he had lost her name.

He rode with his back to the mountains going blue in the dark coming on. A light was burning. He needed to reach it. He rode holding to the horn of his saddle. He did not ride so much as hang there as in some shoddy western. He felt the heat of his face. His face was on wrong. The wind pressed against his back and made him cold.

Her name was Prairie. Prairie was his girl. His wife was what? The wind parted his horse's mane and blew it eastward. The pronghorn would outrun the fire but cattle would heap against fences until the fire burned them alive. The prairie was short-grass prairie. Land of his youth. Blood country.

His horse walked calmly and the flames moved off from them and ash made the going quiet. He slept he did not know how long before his horse spooked and started. A rabbit bounded through the burnt grasses, wind lifting and twisting its hair. Somewhere a bird dipped past. A clump of roots flared.

·

He did not wake again until the ranch house. He had been in the mountains, he explained, pushing cattle. It was a young horse. He did not know any more. He had a wife he knew, could he call her? He didn't know how to call her. He had forgotten the number. Town was hours. He had parked his rig somewhere. Somebody else had been with him. He could not bring up her name, he meant his wife's name. His head was breaking. He was vomiting between words.

He said, I think my name is John. He tried a number. It was somebody else. He had lost his sons' names, his mother's. He tried a number. I think I am John, he repeated.

·

At last he reached her. Elaine was her name. She came to him, a good woman, and nursed him the years in bed. He had been thrown, he supposed. Maybe his horse had reared up and hit him.

He lay in bed for years and tried to think of it. He flew into rages. He had seizures. The doctors worked on him. His jaw had been thrust into his brain. His mind wasn't right, it would not be right again. He could hear his eyes rolling in their sockets. He was dangerous, the doctors told his wife. His wife was thin and weak and her hair fell out. You need to do something, the doctors told her. She came at them with a shovel.

He heard mice half an acre away. The sound of opening a bag of potato chips knocked him to the floor. His boy dropped a horseshoe behind him; his face swelled as if struck.

He went nowhere. Bed to kitchen to bathroom. He meant to take his life but something stopped him.

·

He was forty when the horse wreck happened. He was fifty when they brought him out again into the wind of that dry country. What was expected of him, who would recognize him, how was he to behave?

The grass had come back. Sun had whitened the bones against the fences.

He could not run right but he could stand. He could ride a horse, he discovered. That's what saved him. He kept to the plains, to the coulees. He rode anything. He broke colts with his boys. He roped calves at the local rodeo.

In the fall of that year he was thrown by a colt and dragged by his boot from the stirrup. His boy found him. He was living still. The wind tumbled his hat into a coulee. The boy studied his father—the mess of his face, the years ahead. He saw his life spent. He saw his mother with her robe hanging open.

His name was Trinity. His father twitched in the grass. Jackrabbit, coyote—on anything else a man took mercy.

Trinity, he repeated. Goddamnit, pop. I'm your boy, pop. I am your boy and you are John.

swim for the little one first

How nice you could come to visit. See our home, how we live, how the leaves sweep down. The fields green still.

We turned our clocks back. I brought squash in, tossed a sheet across the withering vines. We're to expect a frost once the wind quits, wind from the north, flurries. A chance.

We'll move the rabbits in in the morning, light the stove. Chicory in your coffee, honey how you like. On the radio the news.

Dark falls and the wind comes up and leaves flock out of the trees. I tug windows shut and yet, inside, doors keep sailing open. Leaves shore up in the kitchen. The floorboards buckle and heave.

These old houses. Every wall leans toward the south, toward you, your modest hills, your clemencies of weather.

It can't be easy. It is a distance. Our stairs are steep and narrow. You will never make it up them; you would never make it down. We would have to keep you, as eccentrics keep their reptiles, captive in a tub.

We have the dog you gave us. We have reasonable jobs in town. Sick pool, personal time. Time to travel. I took a lover from the tropical regions once who washed my feet in the sand. Children loved him. He owned a shirt he never wore. He danced, with keening grace, with my Isabel, who has lived so far to be five.

.

Your room is freshly painted. Your bed is your bed you slept in in Kentucky when you were a boy. The sheets are the sheets Mother monogrammed when she took your name when you married.

If you need anything, if you are up in the night. There is the wingback chair to sleep in. Whiskey in the pantry. Pecan cake in the breadbox—your father's favorite, the cake your mother made you.

Our house is yours, naturally.

You need only ask.

I am awake in the night in the yellow room at the top of the narrow stairs. Tap your cane on the stairs—I'm sure to hear it.

.

We keep our boy with us in our bed. Our boy looks like your boy, like my brother. We gave him your name you gave my brother, the name your mother gave you. He is the third Frederick, a grandson at last. Papa, we named him for you.

My lover's name was Artemio.

¿Quieres tomar mi leche? he used to ask.

He danced beautifully, in keeping with the custom of his people. Isabel bent her back across his arm and dragged her hair through the sand.

My brother was Frederick the second.

He skied out of an avalanche that caught you—we've told the story a thousand times. Your ski swung around and put a gash in your leg and by this wound Freddy tracked you. He skied you out of that chute on his back. You were knocked out; you waked in the hospital.

Remembered nothing. You remember nothing of it now. It can't have happened, you insist, even now. He was weak, your boy, he wasn't like you. The second Frederick.

•

We should have named our boy Jack.

Jack the first, Jack the only.

Manuel, we should have named him, Carlito. Gordito—little fat boy.

You should have said, *Freddy, thank you.* Instead you said, *It can't have been you.*

•

In sleep, my brother, my boy at my breast, makes his visits, too. He is not himself but I know it is him. He is not the boy who set the house ablaze, not the boy who sawed the heads off snakes and skewered mice with a pitchfork. Freddy stands at the door until morning, waiting to be seen. He sees nothing. He has no eyes, no mouth, no reason he can speak of to be here.

The trees thrash in the wind. Apples shake loose and drop to the ground—a sound loud enough to wake me.

•

Pachew, you said, and aimed your cane at my girl.

•

Your cane is wound about with electric tape. The shaft is splintered—you fault the dog. The dog was digging at your peas, *how many times?* You broke your cane across its back.

Pachew.

You will have peas at Christmas and pecans and cabbage in your garden still growing.

Here, snow will heap past the window sash. The bears hunker down and the rabbits, and the frogs endure the season frozen solid. Ice pries slate from the rooftop. When snow slides off the roof, and ice, all at once, the house thunders, and quakes on its rubble footing. The dog gnaws at the door, and Isabel cries out.

My girl sleepwalks, so you know. Isabel talks in her sleep. We mustn't wake her—only follow at her heels quietly until she makes her way back to bed.

Isabel is likely to walk to the church next door and swing from the rope in the belfry. The bells startle her—but she can't wake. She is afraid and calls out for me—but she can't see me, she can't hear. I have to hold her to keep her from looking for me as though I am nowhere near.

•

I am near, Papa, not to worry. Only tap on the stairs should you need me.

You have sight in one eye. One leg is shorter. Your joints swell and wear away and you are older of a sudden, eighty soon, tomorrow we'll mark your birthday.

Your boy killed himself on your birthday.

At dinner your wife fell from her chair, asleep. A long way to come and you are tired.

You don't sleep well. You ache in the night. Your friends are dying. You wake with your hand thrown over your face not knowing it is you.

It's your hand, Papa. You can't feel it. Your hand lies across your eyes. You can't move it. It won't come to you what it is.

•

You may hear birds in the chimney in your room. They often catch there. Their feet scratch the flue. No harm.

You'll hear the wind scrub the hill we live on.

You'll hear me. I sleep lightly, I am up in the night. I am in the room above you, awake when the baby wakes hungry, carrying him across the floor.

His first curl is on the shelf and his umbilical knot in your room where you are sleeping. I buried his afterbirth in the garden deeper than the dog likes to dig.

I keep Freddy's old teeth the tooth fairy left. I keep the lamp Mother made from your ski boot that Freddy dumped the blood you lost out of when he brought you down off the mountain.

You bled wildly. By the blood from the wound, Freddy found you, by the stains on the snow, the blood pooling in your boot. That was lucky.

That lamp made Mother feel lucky. Mother drilled a hole through the bottom of your boot and ran a shaft up through it and filled the boot with cement she threaded wire through.

Funny, what you keep, what keeps at you.

I keep a feather I found in Freddy's pocket.

I keep an acorn I kicked the morning Isabel was born, out walking on the dirt road, my water streaming over my knees.

I keep a satin bow from the attic of the house where we lived when Freddy was alive.

·

You paid a bounty on birds when Freddy was alive, on pigeons and the obnoxious grackle; a nickel for every rabbit trapped, a dollar for the brazen weasel who ran across your shoe.

He killed to please you. Freddy got rich trying to please you. He drowned mice by the dozen in a bucket and a mother raccoon in a wheelbarrow and the last sorry runt of a puppy your bird dog dropped in the barn. The pup wouldn't amount to much—you had him kill it. Freddy blasted the daubed nests of swallows with their spotted eggs inside.

You taught him what to kill, what to run off, to save.

What Freddy killed he put to rest with great ceremony, with flute song, in a common grave, quietly, secretly weeping.

Spare the songbirds, you taught him, for their pleasing song— the plain and faithful phoebe, the thrush and homely wren. Spare the heron, shoot the goose, kill the cuckoo bird that hides its eggs for other birds to raise.

We ran skunks off. We brought a fox home to save and you shot it.

He needed toughening, you always said so. Freddy needed a keener eye.

My brother was pretty; he was beaten in school. He had been born too soon. His lungs were weak. I tried to be your boy—so Freddy wouldn't have to be your boy. Wouldn't get to, I think I should say.

•

Freddy shot a housecat once, out hunting with you, the first and last time you took him with you.

"He's a hazard," you told Mother.

And gave her the geese it was her job to pluck and the pheasant and the dove. Birds are stacked top to bottom in your freezer—pinkish, yellow, their feet still on, more birds than you will eat in a lifetime. Mother plucked the birds on the bottom of the stack and stacked on these are the fresher kill, the birds your next wife plucked for you, bright mallards and drakes, their heads loose on their necks, their feathers carried off by the wind.

•

My lover called me *la flaca*, the skinny one.

I liked the smell of him, and his mighty arms. I liked a little how easily he would accomplish nothing.

He had a scooter we rode around on on sand roads, through tiny towns. He rode me out to see a tribe of monkeys. One stole my necklace. One unlaced my shoes.

Those monkeys were the greedy kings of that town, the *pendejos*, the thugs. They chased dogs off. They stole wallets—stole mine—snatched anything loose.

"Why did you bring me here?" I asked him.

"To teach you to live, *mi flaca,* with nothing."

•

He lived in a lean-to of lashed-together palm fronds. The floor was sand. He had a bucket and a bed. He had a rag he dried my feet with. All night, I could hear the sea.

All night, certain nights, I knew he would kill me. He had strength he wasn't using.

He would scalp me, pretend to be me—my mind blasted clean, ecstatic, swinging my yellow hair.

•

Here is how Freddy went about it: he made a blow dart with straight pins and bamboo and climbed, wheezing, into the hayloft. By dinner, he was hivey, dripping, blotched. He couldn't eat for sneezing.

You have forgotten this. *It wasn't so,* you say. But, Papa, it was.

For hours Freddy lay in the hayloft waiting for the pigeons you hated, waiting for the kill. I liked to watch him. My brother was patient. I saw a snake go over his neck once. He was good at keeping still.

Freddy gave me his old dog you hated—his stuffed dog, old Snoopy dog. He gave it up to me for your birthday.

He didn't need it: he wasn't a kid anymore. He loved it foolishly. You were sure to take it from him; he took it from himself. The dog's big head drooped and swiveled: the stuffing had gone out of its neck.

It smelled awful, my husband insisted, but to me it smelled like Freddy and the bed that Freddy slept in in the house where Freddy died. And so I kept it.

·

I keep the satin bow I meant to give you.

I keep the shell Artemio gave me.

He gave me little; I asked little. He wanted money and I gave it to him. I gave him a shirt and shoes.

He has two shirts now and one ragged bucket—to wash sand from the feet of his women he brings to his lean-to to bed.

·

Nothing stops you. You hunt and fish and travel.

You are buried by an avalanche and your dead boy digs you out.

You keep moving, marry again, keep your hair, your pornography, it can't be easy but here you are. Come to visit. Come to see at last your grandbaby, a little man to carry on.

He is Freddy but not like Freddy—this one loud and plump and strong. Not a quitter.

Don't be a quitter.

"Where's my mister?" you say.

"Where's my water?"

Sit tight: here it comes.

Here comes your boy to save you, digging in from above. You won't even need to thank him—only lie there. It is all you can do.

Bleed, and maybe he'll find you. Breathe. Except the heat from your breath melts the snow against your face. The snow freezes to ice. It makes a mask of ice. That's what kills you.

•

Except it doesn't.

You live to be eighty. You could live to be a hundred and eighty, your grandchildren buried, your new wife dead, sitting in a wingback chair.

Carry on, is your counsel. *Don't be a quitter.*

You stashed food for a year in the basement of our house, taught us to divine for water, to forage for windfall apples under the ice and snow. You taught us the stars to go by and which snakes were safe to catch and how to gut and skin. How to read wind and cloud for weather. How to make an arrow true.

We lit fires with flint how you taught us. Learned our roots and berries. We'd snare rabbits, shoot geese. We'd know mushrooms, cache food. Train a pigeon to carry messages to Mother.

•

Mother, we live in a tree house now the phoebes are happy in. We have water. We know a cave very near and kill rabbits. There is plenty here to do.

•

Chipmunks eat at the walls of our house. A bear rubs its back against the clapboards: that's how it sounds. But that is only the arborvitae, Papa, pressed against the house by wind. Not to worry.

Of course you worry. You stop breathing in your sleep. You find your hand across your face. Your wife has to wake to wake you, so spent she falls out of her chair.

You wake gasping. Your mouth is grainy and dry. Your feet are such a long way from you, bleeding into the snow: not yours.

They are too old to be yours. You can't feel them.

Papa, sleep.

Let yourself rest. We'll have a party for you tomorrow, a nice meal. I'll spend the day in the kitchen.

Isabel wants to hang streamers for you and have a water slide and balloons. She wants cupcakes and rainbow sprinkles. All her bunnies can come.

•

We will take a walk when you wake.

I'll show you the fort my Isabel built with apples and yellow leaves. Our apples were sweet and wormy this year; all but the last have dropped from the trees. They lie in the grass, two tiny bites taken from them. Into two soft apples, Isabel pushed two sticks to stake her rabbit by. I'll have to show you. He wears a collar like a cat. She gets him tied up, the apples at his sides, to watch her, *you have to watch me*, jumping rope in the sun on the church steps, singing jumping songs, singing *rabbit.*

•

Freddy brought you a bird at a party once. He was blotchy and proud. "Here I got one, Papa."

"You dummy," you called him, it's true.

You held the bird by the neck to show the others, the silver pin still in its breast. Everybody had a good laugh at my brother: he had killed a mourning dove, not a pigeon.

Freddy whacked that bird against the side of the barn until its insides were coming out.

•

Freddy killed every bird he could get to after that, didn't matter, every beetle and snake and rodent, and brought them to me as a cat does, and with him a stick to hit him with. Freddy wanted all the wrong things, I knew. I hit him. I did what he asked me. I hit him until we both felt better.

I helped him light a fire with his socks. Because he had lost his coat. This was later. You had had to buy him a new coat and he had lost it and we were afraid of what you would do.

So we lit a fire in Freddy's closet. We would say the coat was burned up in the fire. It wasn't Freddy's fault. His coat was hanging right where it was supposed to hang. There was a fire, we'd say. We were in the barn, we'd say. We didn't know the first thing about it.

.

Here is how Freddy went about it: he fed the ladder through the open window.

It never mattered to Freddy how hard a thing was once he had the idea.

He used the apple-picking ladder, tapered at the top for going up among the branches, and wider as you went down. He climbed a ladder with the ladder on his back—it would never have made the turn on the stairs.

I went up there to look for a bow for you for the gift I had gotten for your birthday. I wanted a yellow bow. I wanted paper with purple dots. I have no idea what I meant to give you only how I meant to wrap it.

There were paintings tacked to the rafters of that house that Freddy and I had painted: volcanoes the lava spat out of, a black and white smiling cow. He painted lightning, pyroclastic flow.

The sun blazed in the attic windows. Flies knocked against the glass, stupid in the cold that was coming. The cold made a fringe of ice on the pond and the last apples swung in the wind in the trees and rotted in the bent-over grass.

He had no shoes on. I thought: he's lost them.

His feet were red from the cold from coming through the grass to feed the apple-picking ladder through the window. He didn't care how hard. Freddy was stubborn. He had a feather in his hat. He lashed the ladder to his back to use his hands to climb—no way could he have made it up those stairs.

The geese were moving. The bears were drunk on apples.

The sun made buttery squares at that hour against the chimney where the ladder had fallen. Freddy kicked the ladder out when the time came. It had rained and his feet were muddy and the sun threw his shadow against the brick.

I stood under him. His foot crossed under his other foot like the feet of Christ in pictures. He sort of turned in the wind. I thought to hit him. I was wearing my pleated skirt.

I sat a long while at the window up there with Freddy at my back and looked out. A few apples hung in the trees still where the branches were too weak to climb. The trees were young still. We had to go to our knees to mow under them.

That became my job, a boy's job. The sky heaped up behind me. The storms came in from the west in that house over the fruitful hills.

•

Hear that?

My husband laughs in his sleep. He wakes himself up laughing.

Otherwise you can forget he is here.

.

Once a cowbird flapped out of the chimney in your room. Its wing was broken. A cowboy bird, Freddy called it.

It's funny what you remember, funny what you forget.

Once a bear came and ate the bees—left the honey, ate the bees. Pulled the bird feeders down, drunk on windfall apples.

.

I get out of bed with the baby and carry him across the room. He nearly glows, looking up at me, his face so plump and pale.

My husband has left his shoes in the middle of the room. It has been raining and his shoes are muddy.

He's still laughing. The owl starts up in the orchard. The leather splits and the toes turn up. He doesn't sound like any man I know.

Count your blessings, Mother always said: he doesn't wake himself up screaming; he is a happy drunk; he dreams funny dreams; you can forget he is even here.

.

That owl. We have barn owls, horned owls, eagles. *Owl* is a funny word.

That's a barn owl, calling across the field. I leave our ladder stood up in the tree the owl likes and, nights I can't sleep, climb toward him. He holds himself very still.

If he has flown, I won't know, you can't hear them. I could knock right into him. Sometimes my knees give out. It is unnerving: to be seen so clearly by something you can scarcely see.

•

Pachew, pachew, pachew, you said, and aimed your cane at my children.

•

Freddy was barefoot; his feet were muddy. One foot went over the other as if to stand in the air on himself.

•

After my brother died, a red-tail attacked you. You were riding your spotted mare, who threw you. The hawk went after your eyes.

You had a red-tail stuffed and the head of a moose. A turkey, a small bear. You had hooves of elk made into ashtrays with a skinny fringe of hide. You had a pair of geese hollowed out and stuffed, lifting off, friends for life. A gift to yourself on your birthday.

Your boy killed himself on your birthday. That is punishment enough for many lifetimes. For this, you don't need me.

•

I'll make a fresh cake. Corn pudding, how you like, and collards. I'll soak a ham. Maybe I'll polish your shoes how I used to.

We'll sing a pleasing song—your wife and I, and Isabel. That's the trick: sing a pleasing song. Dress yourself up pretty.

Let me know what you hope for for your birthday, Papa, something small, a watch, a wallet. Soap on a rope—the old standby. A gleaming golden cane.

Only ask for it.

If there is anything you want—someone will get it for you.

My daughter will. Your wife will, or I will. Somebody always has.

merengue

Everybody had something. They had some black story they were hiding or couldn't wait to tell. They were ballerinas with vertigo, surgeons with busted hands. They'd outlasted the camps, outrun the bulls. They were Green Berets and blind jewelers. They had flown to Paris and Rome.

Now they went about on tricycles and wheelchairs, the want to drift still in them. The old women played bridge and bickered by day and by nightfall slept with the louvers pinched shut. The old toms howled on the beach at night. The old men fished with kittens.

The sea rose up with the tides each year and washed through the lobbies of the old hotels and down the wide fine boulevard. It had been a wide fine boulevard and the beach had been wide and bright. Then starlets arrived in gold lamé with their hair heaped up on their heads. Beauties beyond believing. Now that was over. The young went elsewhere. The sea ate at the beach. Hotels were looted, emptied out but for squatters with their shopping carts and rags.

Now mornings after the water swept through, old men appeared in knee socks swinging their metal detectors. They worked by phalanx, like the organized blind, transistors in their shirt-front pockets. Some could walk still. Others slumped in their chairs. They found little and hoarded it fiercely. Ace found a spoon, a rusted bracelet. Ikey found a *sol* from Peru. What they found, they wagered at cards at night, drunk on *caña* in the hotel lobby. The rats jumped from palm to clattering palm. Small boats gasped in the shallows.

The months went on and on this way in the trick of a season unchanging. The old Jews browned to leather at the high white wall, their tattoos from the camps dimming in their darkening skin. The Hasidim came on Saturdays in their heavy skirts and coats and walked in the water with their shoes still on. The ballerina bought a carrot, a potato, a leek, and made soup with the same soft bone. The cats kept at it. The wind wore at the beach. Somebody got clubbed in the head with a bat. Somebody went off to the morgue.

·

They arrived one bright still afternoon, a day too hot to breathe. They were young and leggy and drifting. A spectacle, an insult. They would make their mark and move on.

They had come from the land of head-high corn, wind in the elms, stone fence posts. Their faces looked milky and wounded. Mary touched her face whenever she spoke as if to hide something wrong with her mouth or what she intended to say. She leaned into Jack as if exhausted, her little skirt riding up, her skin so pale it was blue. She was pregnant; she left the button of her skirt popped open. When she was resting, she slid her hand under her shirt and rubbed her round smooth belly.

They were at the beginning of something, the bright wide life desired.

Yet Jack slept all hours and she wandered. He let her wander— as if nobody would club you in the head for a dime or cut out your kidney with a car key. As if to be young went on forever.

When he wasn't asleep, Jack fished from the pier where the old men dozed and gossiped. He brought a cooler—ice and beer and soda pop—and threw the empties into the water, corked, with the words of some song stuck in them. He wrote music; he could play anything with a string. He had been fa- mous, briefly. The Dutch loved him. But he had ruined his hand punching a calcimine wall and now he rarely so much as hummed.

Jack gutted the fish and threw the guts to the birds, thrusting his thumb up the ditch the bones made. He didn't eat fish, he never had. But he brought the fish cleaned to the hotel room and cooked them, their tails arching up as if alive.

.

Jack slept soundly, the sleep of the dead. His breath whistled in his throat as he slept. The old toms squalled in the sandlot.

Their window gave onto the sandlot, onto the open sea. At night the sea looked greasy, warping in black polished swells. The old Jew living above them let his shoes drop through the louvers at night. Mary dropped fish through the louvers—to give the cats something to fight about, to go ahead and tear each other up about. Old toms. Old scabby, ratty warriors.

She hooked her thongs on. Mary made her way down the car- peted hall rutted by the wheels of shopping carts and thought, *cartwheels*. She never learned. On the beach she tried tossing her legs up and balancing on her head, skull cupped in the cooling sand. Then Ikey walked past with his popping bones and took hold of her ankles. That was helpful. If she stood on her head long enough, the baby would fall into her mouth.

She took the elevator down to the lobby. The only light in the lobby was the fish tank light aerating bubbles streamed through. It made the old men green and viscous. They looked painted, squinting at cards, the shadows of fish thrown across them. The bottle of *caña* was out on the table and the lousy wagers of the last big swell. Ash at their feet, and the divets of ground-out cigarettes.

Mary kissed them each on each cheek—Ikey and Ace and Mel.

Ikey poured her a glass of *caña* and patted the chair next to his chair. He lighted her cigarette.

Her palms were burning: by now she was months along. A stain the color of cocoa had bloomed at the back of her neck. She ate crackers and mashed bananas. Rice and potatoes— white food—white toast floating in milk.

Even with the button popped open, her little skirt scarcely fit. She needed clothes but they had no money for clothes. Jack had insured his hands but that money was spent. If he watched you too long, something ate at your face. He saw wolves crouching in bathtubs. Babies belly-up in the waves coming in, their enormous eyes eaten out.

"He won't touch me," Mary said, "he can't stand to. Poor Jack."

He closed himself in and slept. Fished, slept, ate plantains.

The old men said they would catch him out and thrash him until he cried. He would have to promise to be good to her.

"Fly right," Ace said, and winked at her, and tried to remember what it felt like to touch her, any of them, anywhere at all.

Ace wore the hat of professional men going to work in the forties, the shadow of its brim fallen over his eyes. He wore neckties—narrow and dated and dulled. His teeth were perfect but they were not his teeth. He had been a talk show host and he was talky still. He had talked his way out of the poorhouse, out of matrimony and jail.

Ikey was the expert at marriage: he had been married seven times. He wore his wedding ring still from his latest wife and the ring from his college fraternity. His prostate was the size of a tangerine but he was letting it run its course. A worm worked itself out of his elbow. Let him dance, he said, and he'd be happy. Bachata, merengue, the cha cha cha. *Gracias, señorita.*

Mel thanked no one, there was no one to thank. Maybe God, if he'd had His blessing. Mel went about in a wheelchair. He could walk, but he didn't want to.

Mel let his lip sag, tuning his radio to the gospel station, and the underwater light looked to fill it. He chewed tobacco and spat on the floor in great streaks. He let his thumbnails grow long. He filed his teeth to points. It had been Mel's idea to fish with kittens.

"We could listen to something else," Ikey suggested. "For Mary, for a change. We could dance."

But Mel kept to the gospel station, his radio tuned in his shirt-front pocket. Reception was poor; the music came and went. As the night wore on, the music synchronized with the flux of light from the fish tank, the squalling of cats outside.

They talked of ball games, aches and pains, women they knew or saw on TV. Food, and a can of Coors on a hot day, and how often they had to take a leak.

Mary sat quiet and rubbed her belly. She was groggy and her mind drifted. She had studied her baby in its earliest stages and could picture the egg unmoored, lodged in the starry placenta. There the cells began their long division—eroding vessel, schooling in the bloody lakes. A week, then three, and the head bowed over an open mouth. A puny tail sprouted.

She rubbed her belly. It was a fetus now. You could almost see it was human. It could have been a bear or a mouse until now. A chimpanzee in a zoo.

A whale had fingers in its pectoral fins now, sometimes vestigial legs. It had been doglike once, with hooves like a cow. The platypus was cousins with the zebra—was that true?

Everything ran together, was the truth. All the animals, the living and the dead. The land had been sea and the sea what? And the cornfield sea they had come from.

And here she was. But Mary wasn't here quite. She had slept in her bowl in the sun too long with the dizzy ballerina.

A shadow passed over Ikey's mouth and Mary thought she might throw up. The room moved like a boat; she felt her feet float up. The whole peninsula would break away before long and smash into something else. Geologic time—unimaginable. "Stretch your arms out," Jack said. "That's geologic time."

Jack swiped a file across her littlest fingernail and said, "I just wiped the human race out."

·

He said, "Let's go until we can't go anymore."

He meant land and time and distance. They rode a bus all the way from Kansas, at the seaboard turning south. The air warming and wet and the lights never quit and then they were on a bridge in the dark and a great white bird flew up—a heron, or an egret, unbelievably white in the headlights. Mary had never seen anything so pretty. Then it was feathers, struck, nothing, gone.

Ikey was going on about his prostate. Ace had a nephew in Iowa the boy's mother had spoiled stupid. Little fat boy. He wasted his youth at the computer, twitching and eating Skittles.

"What a kind of life is that?" Ace wanted to know.

The kid ought to be out catching snakes but the snakes were gone. A few lizards were left, a catfish or two in the pond.

"Buy the kid a ball," Ikey agreed.

"Fat chance," Ace said.

Mel said nothing. He had said nothing for years. He made a noise now and then when a woman came near—Mary, or the ballerina on tiptoe. Mel had filed every one of his teeth to a point. He had eaten his tongue down—it took him years—to a ragged stump. Now he couldn't say a word if he had to.

"Mel has his reasons," Ace said. "I think we all do."

"Pair of queens," Ikey said.

"Full house."

•

Jack was alone when he waked and the old Jew was throwing his clothes out the window upstairs. He threw his lamp out, the cord following like a tail. He threw his chairs out, his bed-sheets. The mattress stuck in the window frame and then he sat on the floor and howled. The last lone roaming dog howled back.

Mary would come back.

Jack would never see her again.

She was drowned.

She had been bludgeoned by the prop of an outboard, the boat blasting out through the shallows.

No. She would come back. She had sand on her feet. She would smell of rusting iron, of an animal freshly killed.

.

Jack was sitting on the dresser when Mary came back carrying her dime store thongs. It was morning; the waves lifting out of the sea in the low crisp sun caught fire. Glitter of gulls. Not a body on the beach.

She said, "I dreamed he cut me, here to here."

Throat to cunt, what it looked like. Mary tapped at herself with her shoes.

There was a time Jack thought they would marry but that time was behind them now. He had wanted to know why and thought of reasons. Because he punched the wall. Because the corn didn't make. Mary brushed her teeth sitting on the toilet. No.

They were never going to get any better.

"Who cut you?" he could ask her, but he wouldn't.

A pod of minnows ignited in the face of a wave. Already the day was blazing. Jack would spend the afternoon fishing, see what he could drag out.

Mary hooked her braid over her pillow. Her braid was sandy and her skin looked fried.

When had Jack seen her last? She had been lying in a bowl she had dug in the sand with the dizzy ballerina, slices of cucumber over their eyes.

She said, "I thought he was after the baby, but he was only warming his hands."

"So you slept then," Jack said.

"Yes. Briefly."

"But the wind woke you up. And the cats must have come."

"You were sleeping," Mary said.

"Ah, Jack. All in. Old handy Jack."

"Don't say that," Mary said.

"Say, Jack Handy is a handy Jack."

Funny his name was Handy. He had known a guy named Johnny Fingers, a guitarist, too, back in the day. Wonder what happened to him.

"You were sleeping," Mary said.

"People sleep nights, doll."

"You didn't used to."

Mary reached for him.

"Quit," Jack said. "Have you seen yourself?"

Her skin looked puffed and crazed from the sun. Her braid looked like something living.

"You're all burned up. Who could touch you?"

"And if I stayed in out of the sun?" Mary asked.

Jack knocked the sand from her braid. Jack Handy.

"Jack?" she insisted. "It's as easy as that?"

·

What was easy? Exactly nothing.

"I can't stand this," Jack said. "I hate living here. It's like a nursing home without nurses."

"We could go somewhere else."

"We can't," he said.

Jack used to count to himself, during: come to ten, count back, count evens, odds—the beats of the slow nosing-in Mary liked, the jab at the end: nothing to it.

In his mind he saw curlews swooping, their specked eggs wobbling in the corn. Mary's hair cut short—boy's hair. He sort of liked that. Her face above him, her green eyes mostly closed.

He saw Kansas, the darkling plain.

He liked places better than people. Great dark swaths. Quiet. The sound of the wind in the corn, he liked.

They hacked paths through the corn when the sun was high and rooms to pass the night in, setting out from the house with a basket of food, a little junk to snort, whiskey. They found a burst mattress they dragged there. The walls rustled and the moon threw shadows.

Because the corn didn't make.

Because nothing. Because Mary couldn't sing, not even baby songs.

She wanted babies.

Because Jack shared a bed with his sister until he was seventeen.

She drank his coffee. She brushed her teeth on the pot. She sucked her thumb when she was tired.

Because he was tired of her.

Because he was tired.

Summer came and went, Mary counting the days. She stretched her legs above her head and still nothing.

Jack counted evens, odds. He was gentle. Handy, patient, gentle Jack. Then she was pregnant, but only briefly.

He took her gently at first in the night heat one night she was months along, believing he could not harm her. Her body softened; she seemed to pool in the bed. She had drowned in her hair, her spalling bones. Jack was methodical, exalted, weeping. He moved through her, breathing out his name.

Then nothing. Because of nothing.

They waked in bloody bed sheets.

Because he touched her. He couldn't touch her.

Jack never did want babies. He didn't know it until theirs was gone.

The nights grew cool. The cranes started south; it made her restless. At first Jack got himself out of their bed and followed her where she went. *Everywhere that Mary went*—even baby songs she sang off key.

She stopped brushing her hair and wore the same clothes. She slept in her bra and underpants. Mary smelled of the ash of the burned-over fields the cranes came to to feed on.

Because of that.

Because of that.

Because the cranes kept pace with the flame, Jack remembered; they drove their beaks at the band of heat where the insects popped and flared—great lanky squabbling flocks gorging themselves for the flight from the north, from the ice, the polar quiet.

·

People came down here for quiet?

Nothing doing: they came to see the same day repeated. Salt wind, unabating heat. The tranquilizing beat of the sea.

The mind softened. Birds appeared. The gossipy palms repeated themselves.

Mary dug a hole in the sand each day to lie with the ballerina in. The ballerina was older than all of them. Her skin sagged from her knees like an elephant's. She had lipstick smeared on her teeth.

Ikey limped past in his knee socks. The old Jew threw his crap from his window at night and gathered it up by day. Day in, day out. Sometimes the water rose up. That was something.

The old Jew went out and the ballerina came in: that meant the day was over. He was a creep but it didn't matter.

Why didn't it matter? Jack couldn't say.

The old Jew dragged his chair across the sandlot where he threw his lamps and shoes and folded it out beside the hole where Mary lay with cucumbers over her eyes. He had numbers on his arm from the camp he'd been in. Jack could see it all from the window. The chair was webbed and the webbing had frayed and the old Jew looked to hang out of himself when he sat down in it.

He got his pants open and spit in his hand. He shook out a plastic shopping bag to hide himself and went at it. Sometimes it took a while. The day was over; the lights on the boulevard came on. When his body bunched up and his feet turned in, that meant he had finished his business. He was collecting seed for future Jews: every day he twisted his bag shut and carried it back to his room.

Mary lay there still.

Why didn't it matter?

Maybe he was quiet and Mary couldn't hear him.

Maybe he whimpered and moaned.

·

The old men had heard the sea so long they could no longer hear it.

It was like listening to your liver work: you had to really want to do it. Your heart, your wife, the wind; the worm working out of your elbow. When it stopped—that was when you heard it. Maybe, maybe not.

It was getting harder to catch things, even with kittens and a snelled hook. The old men hooked kittens through the backbone and fished off the long pier. They dragged sharks in, the lesser demons that cruised the shallows. The meat tasted like bleach but they ate it.

Mel ran his share through the blender and doctored it up with lime. The gospel hour wouldn't come in, or came in only sometimes, bursting from Mel's shirt-front pocket. The wheels of his wheelchair needed oil but it wasn't worth the fuss. He squeaked about, reeking of *caña*. He had reeked of *caña* for forty years.

Ace drank, but not the way Mel drank. He could tell stories about Mel he wasn't telling, stories Mel had eaten his tongue not to tell. Still Ace banged on, and stroked his fresh grosgrain hatband with the feather of a rare bird in it.

Ikey's prostate ran its course. The cells divided; the gland enlarged. The cells would make their way out of the sack soon but Ikey refused to believe it. He meant to live until Mary's baby came so he could be the baby's jolly uncle.

Ikey had never been anybody's uncle. He had been a father a dozen times—twelve sons, not a girl in the bunch. He wanted daughters. Fresh wives. He liked women, but they never did seem to last.

He liked to walk Mary down to the cut, afternoons, to watch the big cruise ships go by.

"Where would you go if you could go anywhere?" they asked.

Mary would go by horse or on foot. She didn't know where. It didn't matter to her.

Ikey said, "I would go back forty years myself and ask you to marry me please."

"Third wife of eight," Mary figured. "What else?"

"I'd paint your toenails and buy you ice cream."

"Nice."

"Feed you chocolate mousse with a spoon. I'd fly you off to Paris, France, and kiss you on the bridge above the river. The pigeons would roost on our windowsills and in the morning a girl in a flowered skirt would bring fresh bread to our room. I'd float roses in the tub. I'd buy you all the clothes you wanted and make love to you in your pretty new dress in a booth at the opera house."

"You've done all that."

"Not with you."

Ikey slid his wedding band off his finger for Mary to hang on a string around her neck.

Jack wouldn't notice.

Of course he would.

A bunch of boys pulled up in the parking lot and opened the doors and let the radio play. Cumbia, merengue, salsa—Ikey could dance them all. He would teach Mary; he would count out the steps.

They danced; sometimes she stood on his feet, her belly pressed against him. Her hair smelled like fruit or candy. Ikey thought of his boys and his grandkids, grown. His boys had children, wives, houses in faraway places. He had lost touch with them. *Lost touch* is how we say it.

Mary wore a T-shirt over her bikini and the strings were hanging down. Ikey wound a string around his finger. He could tug it and see what he wanted. He wanted her bikini to drop out of her shirt so he could see her breasts against it. That was all. He wouldn't touch her. He would want to but he wouldn't do it.

Unless she let him.

Suppose she let him.

Old fool. Old stupid, useless wanting.

Mary had been swimming and her bikini was wet still and it dampened his shirt when they danced. They were dancing with their feet in the water. Her voice moved in her neck and Ikey felt it. He was dying—he could feel that, too. He was an old man dying on the seashore and the sun was like a hand against his back.

·

It was dark when Ikey and Mary got back and the lights were on in the hotel in every window but hers. Jack had gone out. Nobody asked where.

Ace and Mel were down in the lobby. The ballerina went through on tiptoe in a little flowered skirt and fresh lipstick. Mel made the sound he made—like a dog lying down to sleep. He showed his teeth; his teeth looked like a joke. The ballerina tried to smile at him but she couldn't get her face to move. She tiptoed to the fish tank and held on to the rim for balance.

The fish were drowning. They were choking in the murk. The ballerina stood on one foot and drew her other foot slowly up her leg. She had great turnout. Her skin was like a second set of clothes. She broke crackers into the water; the crumbs fattened and sank.

"*Gracias, señorita.*"

Ikey spoke for the fish. Other people speak for the trees.

Mel spat a speckled stream of tobacco juice and tugged on the ballerina's skirt.

She went out. She had no use for them. She had a sweetheart she drank Campari with who kept her in Botox and shoes. She had shoes she never wore, a beaver coat. She was a countess but the proof was muddy.

They played cards and drank and when Mary felt a little drunk, she brought a bottle of Clorox down and a toothbrush to scrub the algae off the shipwrecked plastic boat.

"What's the difference between a ship and a boat?" Ace asked.

They had heard it before but they pretended they hadn't.

"A boat is what you get on when the ship is going down."

The one fish with the prettiest tail had already eaten at some of the others.

Ikey unwound a hanger for her and Mary cut the toe of a stocking off and with this she scooped up the prettiest fish—because it was the prettiest fish. Because it ate other fish for fun. Mary scrubbed the tank clean and filled it and every time Mary looked at Mel, he showed her his ragged tongue. It hardly looked like a tongue. It was lacey and gray. Mel chewed a piece loose and dropped it into the tank and the prettiest fish went at it.

"Good Christ," Ace said, "keep your tongue in your mouth. Nobody wants to see it."

Mel rolled his chair close to Mary and took her by the neck. He brought her face to his face as if to eat it and Ikey dumped him out of his chair. Mel lay on the floor moaning.

"Get up, you shit. Quit suffering," Ikey said.

"Somebody ought to knock him in the head," Ace said.

Mel got quiet and quit moving. He looked molded, flung into the green of the fish tank light. Ace kicked him softly.

"He loves to suffer," Ace said. "There's no fixing him. You have to forget he's alive."

Mel didn't look alive much. Spit hung from his mouth. Soon he held out his hand to be helped up and Mary made a move to move toward him.

"Don't do it," Ikey said, and she didn't.

"A woman married him once," Ace told her. "Hard to believe but it's true. She was the homecoming queen, pretty and smart. He about killed her. Slow. Just from suffering. By and by Mel drove her out so he could suffer that, too. Just for gusto. I don't get it. I have been knowing Mel Carson most of my life and I do not begin to get it. He had parents but you'd think him an orphan. You think he's broke but his pants are crammed with money."

Ace took a big swig of *caña*. He was on a roll and he liked the feeling.

"It's in the genes," Ace went on, "that hangdog head, that mopey slump. Public sufferers. You can't change that. He's got two good legs; he rolls around in a chair. First People. Mel's people feed on moping. Little urchins, wincing along on their blisters. You're new, you just moved, but they find you. Look! Some punk with a rusty mower, dragging a snaggled rake. Some stammering prince with a briefcase, shaking the change in his slacks. Tie tied wrong, belt cinched tight; kid's nursing two kinky, flimsy hairs from the seep of his pimply chin. He'll sharpen your knives, level your hedge, polish your hubcaps, you name it. 'Why not give yourself the gift of beauty?' he asks. 'Lotions, liners, powders, salts. A lift, a tuck, a plumper breast. A pair of cement lions. Seen it before? Here's something new: an electric windshield scraper, a Water Pic that sings.' He's slick. He'll say you saw him coming—smart. 'I'm on your street, I climb your stoop. A guy like me, I'm easy, a scrapper, check the doors. But what am I saying, lady? Lady, please, forgive me, I'm wasting precious time. You're practical, no doubt. No doubt you watch your budget. No foolishness, no frills. Maybe Mrs. Pewee, Mrs. Bliss, they'll buy. Water Pics and whatnot. Gewgaws for the yard. So, look, love, I say, dandy. But this crap is not for you! Gadgets, trinkets, amusing for a time. I say, Melvin, Melvin, skip it, quit—they're for the Mrs. Blisses, the Treseders, the blind. But for you, for you, a woman like you, I have books for the kids and bibles, mausoleums, soap—black soap, soap that floats, liniment, balm. Land, land, a sportsman's dream, a dream for all the ages. For the hungry, the orphaned, the oft-forgotten old. Profits for the planet, miss. Greeting cards for cancer, the walking dead and wounded, the kindygarter trip to the zoo.'"

Ace was slowing down, ceasing. His hands shook and his face felt slack. His tie pulled tight around his neck.

"You finished?" Ikey said.

"Christ Jesus." If Ace leaned back, his chair would go over. "Sell you fifty damn cents for a dollar," he said at last, "the way he makes you feel."

Ace didn't want to feel anything. He wanted peace and quiet and *caña* and a quiet game of cards.

Mary helped Mel into his wheelchair. His skin looked luminous, easy to tear. She turned away when she touched him but the feeling of his skin made her sick. He felt slippery, reptilian, the radio in his pocket hot: the last thing living in him. Mary rolled his chair back against the table and went into the street for air.

Ikey dealt Mel in. Ace kept quiet and won the next three hands. They played hearts and Ace tried to shoot the moon but Mel had the queen in his sock. Ace saw it there and said nothing.

Why?

Ace was chicken was why.

He had chosen nothing. Between grief and nothing, nothing. Ace had loved the girl Mel married—so quietly he scarcely knew it himself.

He didn't marry; didn't fight. No survivors. Nobody sobbed in the cloisters for Ace. He had talked himself out of his life.

Now this was life: bottle of *caña*, cards. The same day come around, come around again.

Same question. Which was better—being sorry for a life you never had or sorry for a life you had lost?

Chicken or an egg. Which was better?

Tiger or a mule. Who would win?

Between an ant and a worm?

A boy and a stick?

Between grief and nothing?

What was nothing—this? Three old men, a deck of cards?

Paper, scissors, rock, Ace thought.

An ant because he can eat the worm. A worm because he lives eaten. Lives to eat. No difference? Between your suffering, mine. The life lived, the life not lived. The cradle and the grave.

Where was Mary? If Mary were here, Ace would kiss her.

If paupers were kings. If her baby came. Ace kept seeing himself holding her baby, saying *kikiriki* like a rooster.

No babies for Ace. He would swim if he could. He would sleep for a week and wake in the cold in the snow coming down and the quiet. Quiet. A deer on teacup hooves. That was Ace.

Cheated or a cheat. Which was better?

Would Ace wish his life on anyone, on even Mel who had had his day? His beautiful wife, his house with a pool. His god-like years in high school. Mel had been wicked and handsome and wild. On the move, boy. You couldn't stop him. He got rich off an ad on the television set at a time kids were flipping burgers for cash and tossing newspapers from bicycles. Rich off the soap that floats—that ad. Ivory Soap. So Pure it Floats. Sell you fifty cents for a dollar, Mel. Fuck anything that moved— dorks and dummies, orphans, freaks, chicks in purple lipstick bursting out of their clothes. Women loved him. Mel leaned in, whispered his sorrows in their ears. Suffered his way into their bedrooms.

And then?

And Ace?

And the boy who died? The house with the pool and the boy who died because Mel was too drunk to do anything?

I didn't do anything.

I did nothing.

I didn't want anything.

I wanted nothing.

Between a chicken and a cheat.

Chicken and an egg.

Between the cradle and the grave.

You had the hand you were dealt, the black queen in your sock. Your puffed-up balls in your pocket. Sticky bars and strip joints, vodka cocktails in the sunshine by the side of your sparkling pool. Your boy. A sunny day for his birthday, his pretty mother someplace else. Mel had been drinking since morning the morning before—he had to live with that. Mel was too drunk to see. Or he saw his boy drowning and was too drunk to move. Or he was passed out. Or he sat and watched and did nothing until there was nothing to be done.

You were a cheat or a saint and your life came and went and there was no going back to fix anything. Not anything.

I didn't do anything.

I did nothing.

Nothing to be done.

·

The tides came and went. The stars wheeled through.

Ikey coddled his balls in his pockets.

Maybe he ought to go talk to a doctor after all and see about staying alive. He'd sworn off them, sorry hacks and butchers. They let his heart quit on the table last time and got him hooked on pills.

Still it was common, the prostate, a man of his age. Apparently they thought it was easier to suffer what was common.

Maybe they could shrink it down some. It was a crapshoot; it wouldn't hurt much. "I could give you six months," the doctor would say.

I could poke you in the eye.

Ikey would take Mary somewhere else, given time. He would buy her a skirt that fit her.

"Would you play it?" Ace said, and nudged him.

"Pair of jacks," Ikey said.

"That's nothing."

Mel laid his cards down—he had nothing, too. He rolled his wheelchair to the fish tank and leaned his head against it. Mel could see every fish in the fish tank now and the clean colored marbles and the ship. The plastic Indian in a heap of turquoise. Mel wagged his thumb in the water and the prettiest fish rose to meet it.

He speared fish as a kid and remembered the quiet and how nothing else living was afraid. It was a mistake, of course, not to be afraid. He remembered turtles deep down, asleep in the sand, their faces tucked away in the coral. Just a kid then. What was that like.

Mel pressed his radio against the glass of the tank and watched the sound ripple through the water. The ripples made the fish swim faster. Mel dialed the sound up. The fish bumped against the glass. He dialed the sound louder and the ripples grew and his mother's face came into his mind. What was left of his mind, Mel thought. What a mess he had made of living.

•

When the navy detonated bombs in the sea, whales bled from their brains and beached themselves but it didn't really matter.

Why didn't it matter?

The whales were loaded with PCBs. That didn't matter either, and not cormorants slathered in oil, not turtles burned alive in the Gulf Stream or polar bears that drowned. If the ocean rose up they'd build sea walls and drag every living thing from it, by God.

"God loves humans. Dominion is God's idea, man. Everything here is for us."

Jack didn't know about that. He was drunk but the guy he was drinking with made him look like Mary Poppins.

"Don't be a faggot, man. Drink. You been sipping."

The guy stumbled off to the bathroom and came back with his pants hanging down. Somebody had cut him. He had blood to his knees.

Jack liked a good farm boy fight now and again but he didn't have the stomach for knives. He got out. He was skunked and he couldn't say quite was the sea straight ahead or behind. He tried to sniff it out. The street was spinning. Jack made his way down it. He was alone but he talked to Mary as he went.

They were finished. Surely she could see that. They were killing each other. They were kids.

The doctor had told him not to but Jack would talk to her again about the baby. Jack had gone along with it, how the doctor said, how you go along with a sleepwalker until she walks safely to bed. But it had been months now and Jack was sick of it.

He hadn't touched her since they lost the baby. Or he had done it in his sleep. Or somebody else had.

Jack hadn't known which one to wish for.

Because here Mary was, pregnant again. Immaculate—he hadn't thought of that.

Funny her name was Mary.

Poor Mary. Nobody touched her. Nobody loved her enough. Nobody followed Mary when she went out at night thrashing through the corn.

It was crazy but it wasn't that crazy, Jack thought: it happened with animals, too. Jack had had a dog after all when he was a boy who gave birth to dead puppies in the pantry. They almost lost her. But then she swelled up again weeks later, leaking teats, all the signs, and his sister went blind when their mother died and that was something, too.

The sea was behind him. Jack had his bearings now. He would come upon the little wooden door soon with the tricycle and the shoes.

Mary would be down in the green with the old men and she wouldn't want to come upstairs. But she would have to. Jack was sick of it.

Mary was faking but it wasn't faking.

Her breasts swelled; her belly grew. She read books and the books became instructions: a stain will appear on your neck. Her teeth grew loose; her hair fell out.

Because a stain appeared on her neck, Jack thought.

Because it was like being accused.

Mary wrecked her skin in the sun every day because that was how to grow a baby. It grew sunward. Except it didn't.

A baby needed sunshine not to be born blind: that was Mary's theory.

Salt and sun and water. She had it worked out.

Our Lady of the Sorrows. Sound of the sea. Out of wanting.

But wanting didn't make it so.

•

The old men were still in the lobby when Jack got back to the hotel. They looked up from their cards and got quiet. He had blood on his shirt and his face was a mess.

The boy was a waste of clothes.

"Where's Mary?" he wanted to know. "I need to talk to her."

You need to marry that girl and build her a house with a microwave and a pool, Ikey thought.

Lie down, Jack was thinking. Get level.

He banged his head on the railing tripping going up the stairs.

He had vomited on his shoes. Why had he worn his shoes? That was stupid. He threw them out the window by their laces. They were down with the dirty Jew's now, mildewing in the sand. Down with the cats and the fish bones.

The cats were squalling, a swallowed, liquid howl. They made Jack's skin crawl—old toms creeping through the strangler fig, the grid of the ruined city. They slinked from boxes, from the sweetening throats of culverts—gammers, scrappers, boily hides, old malignant daddies. The gulls went for their balded tails—no match. White rags.

Nothing stopped them.

A plate fell past the window, a flowering brassiere.

Jack pulled his shirt off. The air was gummy; it was too hot to sleep. He wanted to peel himself open and walk about airing his liver.

There was a wad of Mary's hair on Mary's pillow. No Mary. *Your hair will fall out. Your veins will stand up.*

Your sweetheart will run away screaming.

•

Jack slept the sleep of the dead. While he slept a bunch of local boys took turns fucking Mary. They crammed sand in her mouth to keep her quiet. They knocked a tooth loose and Mary swallowed it.

They were boys not long finished with their milk teeth, minors the law couldn't touch. They carried baseball bats and sold candy.

She looked pregnant but that didn't matter to them. She was a girl on a beach and there were four of them and they took her by turns how they wanted with the shortest boy going last, and last again, until Mary quit moving and the moon threw light across the water.

•

She would live but she would never have babies, the doctors said.

"Out of the question."

"Who asked a question?" Ikey asked.

The doctors looked like pansies on a soap opera set. They were too young for what they were doing and they seemed to forget Mary was there.

She mostly wasn't. The boys had gone at her with a bat. She was emptied out and drifting and, when she spoke, sand tore at her throat.

"I lost the baby," Mary said.

Ikey brushed the hair from her face.

"I lost the baby," Mary said. "Who are you?"

.

Mary's clothes had washed up with the tide when Jack waked and the ballerina brought them to him, dripping to his door. Jack didn't know they were Mary's clothes yet. It was noon and he had slept through everything.

His head was pounding. His tongue was a slab in his mouth.

"Where's Mary?" he wanted to know. "What happened?"

But Mary had made them swear not to tell him.

Because Mary had made them swear not to tell him.

Because it was like being accused.

.

It was Ikey who brought her back from the hospital.

Her face was purple still and swollen. The tooth she had swallowed, she shat out. Mary fished the tooth out of the toilet with the net Ikey made with a hanger for her and washed it with soap and kept it. Her skirt fit her again.

She spoke to no one. They could talk to her all they wanted. They couldn't touch her. She could almost not even see them, any of them, if she knew they were going to be there.

Still she went out sometimes to the beach again and lay in the sand at the tide line where the water could almost reach her. She lay with her mouth against the sand. Everything hurt still. They had done a D & C but nothing flushed out but the seed of the boys who had raped her.

She had lost the baby. Nothing else mattered.

"You lost nothing," Jack said.

But she had.

●

Jack fished and slept and ate plantains. He slept when Mary slept and stayed near.

The old Jew left bowls of milk for the cats. The milk was poisoned. The cats' tongues swelled and clogged their throats and the poison ate at them slowly until they were dry as a shoe. Slow. But it was quiet. Then it was over.

Now the old Jew was all Mary heard and the tide moving in or out. He left a dead sparrow in their doorway. Its belly was split; rice bulged inside—somebody newly married. He left Dixie cups of milk. He rubbed his back against their door and meowed at them. There was a hole in the door where the deadbolt had been and he pushed his finger through it. Jack bent it backward. He had to laugh at himself. Jack ought to kill the creep but he couldn't. He couldn't even kill himself.

Jack jerked off in the sink while Mary slept, sun pushing against the louvers. She dreamed of babies with zippers that opened onto other babies, each one prettier than the last. She cut her name into her arm.

"If you need me I am here."

"And if I don't?" Mary asked.

"You will," Jack said.

She was prettier now. Something. Gone. Jack found he wanted her again, who she was now, smaller, damaged, quiet.

He would bide his time, wait her out. Be good to her. Marry.

Meanwhile Jack brought her fried plantains and oiled her feet in bed. He shaved her legs for her. Brushed her teeth for her. There was blood on the sheets when he waked at night but by morning it wasn't there. There was a dog at the door with a mitten. A bird in Mary's hair.

He shit beetles. Still Jack stayed nearby, watching over.

Sometimes Ikey appeared with sweet rolls and a sack of lollipops and a kitten. He was old but he looked even older. Water streamed from his eyes and his head shook. He had stopped clipping the hair from his ears.

"I don't know what to do," he kept saying, stroking the kitten from head to tail.

Mary lay against the wall with the sheet over her head.

"You been fishing?" Jack asked him.

"Nope."

"Bachata?"

"Nope. Nope."

The kitten would give Mary something to care for, to get her mind off herself. Ikey left it on the bed and went out.

The kitten swiped at Mary's hair. It invented another kitten to play with, to pounce and roll around. Mary dropped it through the louvers when Jack laughed at it and pulled the sheet back over her head.

Ikey would come back. That didn't matter to her.

He would carry the kitten upstairs to her again and say, "Mary."

·

Ikey brought fish and a fish bowl for her and a little red barn and a cow. He brought the Indian to Mary from the tank downstairs and the little heap of turquoise. The Indian's paint was off but he was fetching still with his knife and his crooked spear. Mary stayed under the sheet and watched the fish. One had a glistening tail. She hummed a song to it, wordless, of the sea. The Indian tipped slowly over.

Mel was Indian, too, some middle-west tribe with a twelve-vowel name. Starved out, massacred, bought.

The sea had risen up; the streets were flooded. Mel was out with his metal detector, no doubt, gliding down the boulevard. He would bring Mary something—some trinket, she hoped, a gecko swept along in the flood. Mel would wait beside her bed, his knees against her bed, and lean over her. He had warmed his hands in her—but that had been a dream. Now Mary wasn't dreaming. Mel was standing beside her bed; he had left his wheelchair outside their door. He pulled the sheet to the floor and Mary lay there.

There was nothing to her. She was salt, sand, water. His. He could do with her what he wanted.

He could tear her apart with his teeth.

Mary closed her eyes. His breath was hot on her face. His hands moved over her, they were Jack's hands. They were the hands of the boys on the beach. He smelled of *caña*, of salt wind, wind from the south, fish he had cleaned. His radio quivered in his shirt front pocket—flatline. Blown heart—the last of the heat that was in him.

He would seize up soon; the tide would carry him out. A speck in the shine, shine in the eye. Ride the swell in the sunshine, face to the rumbling deep. Heat on your back. Float for a time. The body floats for a time and then what?

He dialed the sound up: static. Now her teeth hummed, her mind shook clean. Mel was trying to tell her something but he couldn't shape the words. His tongue pulsed in his throat, ragged and gray. No words. Vowels. A torrent. He was spitting in her face.

She closed her eyes again. Mel was howling. His boy flailed in the blue of the pool. She couldn't get to him. She had made it all up—no baby, nothing to lose. *You lost nothing.* But she heard it still, still it—what? Howled? Clawed at the wall? Blue of the pool? She was cold. And hot at once and cold. She was lying in the sun and freezing and the sky kept blacking out. There were stars. There were fish with little lanterns gliding by above. Light to see by. Stutter in the bone, sand in her throat. Still she heard her voice, Mel's voice, primitive and churchy, subside and rise again: one cry. But they were a thousand pieces. They were sinking—tiny, ragged flakes—slow through the dark and cold. Nothing to it. Everything here. The beginning and the end, everything here, the last of anything that lived. Mel's boy was here, and Mary's baby. They were food. And Mary was food and Mel was. And the big fish and the little fish, and the day came back around.

•

The day was blazing. It had been a month since Mary had spoken much and she was sick to tears of her room. Sick of Jack and his ministrations. She smelled meaty, raw. Something.

Mary cleaned herself up and went out.

Ikey came out and sat with her and they watched the waves come in. They sat quietly, sun on their backs. Ikey took his shoes off and pointed the toes out to sea. He touched his foot to her foot and she let him. She put his ring in her mouth without thinking, fitted it to her tongue.

"And Jack?" he asked at last.

"Jack's fine," Mary said.

And Ikey was fine and Ace was and Mel was dead and buried. She hadn't known that.

"We're catching up," Mary noticed.

"At last," Ikey said.

He brushed the hair from her face. The ballerina had found a new sweetheart. The cats were coming around again—a fresh batch.

"And Jack?" Ikey asked.

"You asked that."

"And?"

The waves were bringing something shoreward, a darkened patch, a rounded back. Mary moved out toward it, bunching her skirt in her hand.

The waves tumbled the turtle and righted it. Its eyes were open. Brain matter fluttered through the crack in its skull and its flippers were bound in fishing line.

When the tide moved out away from the turtle, they worked at the line with Ikey's pocket knife, the flippers supple still and like satin to touch and they waited for the turtle to move. Blink. Something.

It looked alive but it didn't move. Mary hummed a little—off key, she knew.

The lights on the boulevard came on. It was late now and now vultures came gliding by low with their heads tipped down.

"We should go," Ikey insisted, but she wouldn't.

His strength had left him. He lay on his back in the last of the light and watched the birds, the great gliders, the bright crooked wings of the gulls.

At last Jack appeared with a shovel. They dragged the turtle up the slope until the sand dried out.

Mary did most of the digging. The sand got heavier, wet. There were shells in it still and river silt, not a river in sight but you could hear the sea and Mary thought a little deeper yet would be sand from decades ago—sixty, seventy years ago, the turtle small as a pet store turtle then, small as a child's hand. Mary made the hole deep and narrow: she could see out, but only sky. First star. The waves broke on the shore—temblors, rising through the soles of her feet.

Jack lowered the turtle down to her. Its flippers caught and the head swung up. The flippers were pale underneath like a raptor's wings to hide it in the shine when it breathed. At the hinge was a hooked claw to dig by. Mary dug grooves through the sand with her fingers and the turtle dropped and hung up again, its flippers bent and twisted.

She was in the way of it. It was hanging like something butchered, like a man in a clumsy dance. The flippers pressed against her and the head bent as though to look at her, the fringe of brain white and sodden against the dark shell of its skull. The turtle's mouth was hooked and its tongue showed. It smelled of the cold it had come from. Its eye was going to swing in its socket.

"Stop crying, Mary. This is silly."

"I'm not crying."

"She's crying," Ikey said.

Mary bent her knees and the turtle slipped and when she was up from in the way of it, she pushed it to its belly with her feet. By then she could scarcely see the turtle, the dark of its shell from above. She dug a tunnel for its head and bent the head toward the sea and in the dark the waves felt louder, breaking ceaselessly on the white of the beach, and breaking and drawing away.

today is an early out

Charlie Finch was no bigger than a clothespin. He was walking around on his face. He was farming his face, actually—going from cheek to chin. There was a seed in each blemish on Charlie Finch's face and each seed ate a plum-sized hole through the skin as soon as Charlie popped the blemish open. Flowerettes of cauliflower pulsed in the holes. Except, actually, they were softer. They were lesser, softer corals, Charlie thought. He liked the shine on them. They flinched; they shrank to a dot when he poked them.

Charlie Finch slept a lot and heavily. He was of the age, growing. He liked ping-pong. He liked skating down the hill to school. Girls did nothing for him—what he means is they are, you know—Billy still, or Chuck, or Hank in the case of Hannah. They were still little girls he gave boy's names to back in the fourth grade. He could tell them his dreams and they listened. He could say, "I sleep through everything. I slept through the whole crazy flood."

Except he won't. Before long, you might have heard, before the hour is out, his mother will come up the stairs to wake him. He'll be farming the botched little plot of his face and she will shout his name and shake him and the world Charlie Finch wakes into will prove far stranger than the one he was in. There is time still, a little. Let him sleep, why not. There is nothing to do but warn them.

And there is nothing in a warning that will move them: the Finches have been through this all before. They know their chances.

•

Father Finch is an iconoclast, sort of. A big guy, wide through the chest: *Don't tell me what to do.* The air is cleaner up here against the mountains. He likes the view—their long look down on the city, their patch of the gray Pacific. He swims distances. He saved a kid in a riptide from drowning.

Father Finch is your man for gradients, diversion walls, the angle of repose. He consults with the boys at the Army Corps and rides them to keep the catch clean—the vast basin blasted from bedrock above the court where the Finches live. He lives well, and people like him. They depend on him. Nobody knows his shit better than Finch does. He's been notching houses into the mountainside for going on twenty years.

He designed the family house; he built it. The stem walls are three feet thick and beefed up with miles of rebar. He's got her anchored into bedrock with eyebolts, with braided cable as big around as his boy's arm.

Let it come, Father Finch thinks: *Try me.* His house is a goddamn fortress. It's like a boat that has never been on the water: he wants to see what she'll do.

·

Mother Finch is sweeping. It isn't, you know, that she doubts him, it's just she—well, she hears things. She reads, and reading makes her worry, and worry makes her pinched and brittle— his words—and the creases darken up between her eyebrows, baby, and nothing takes them away. Plus he's smart. She relies on him; she has to. That's how it works between them. Their marriage works, it just does, it's been years. He walks her onto the deck if it's clear and makes her thank him for the view.

Of course, she's grateful, it's just—you know. She has been inside too much or something. She has been ordering hats out of catalogs but she still feels testy and blue. She needs sun, a good dose, it's just been too long, a little California glow.

She's all mixed up. She wants to know things, she thinks, but she doesn't. The rain has drummed down for days—she knows that. They could have built somewhere else—she knows that. She knows the chaparral burned and the dirt up there—well, the Army boys say, she can't fathom it quite—the dirt won't take on water. The brush explodes as though doused with gasoline and the burn runs hot and blue. Fire makes the dirt immune to water. You drop it in a glass and it floats. You drop several inches of rain on it and the whole slope starts to move.

Mother Finch has spent the last hour sweeping. It takes her mind off the rain to clean. She wants to vacuum; she wants to whip up a margarita—but she doesn't want to wake her Charlie. She doesn't want to take the chance.

·

Charlie's sister is up already. Charlie's sister can't sleep for worrying what to wear to school. She has a pleated skirt, but honestly. Aren't pleats too much with your hair in braids? She lets it all back down again. It's kinky. Her hair is stupid. Everything she puts on is stupid. It's impossible to sleep without your clothes laid out. That's the stupidest thing of all.

Can they not call the whole thing off? Call it a rain day. She wouldn't hate that. Kids don't even get out for lunch in the muck and the boys come in with their shoes just soaked and they smell. The whole school smells like skanky sneakers.

Charlie's sister puts her face to the window. The lights do nothing. It's just pathetic. Her dad's pathetic. He's got them blazing away like always but there's nothing but rain to see.

·

Chances are nobody sees it. A boulder wobbles down from the chaparral to the lowlands where the boys from the Army Corps have made a concrete ditch of the stream. It takes a turn into the groove and rolls faster. The boulder is as big as every stitch of clothes Charlie's sister has ever owned—if you think of them all balled up, which Charlie's sister does.

·

Mother Finch thinks bowling—or she will. When she gets a good look at the boulder that plugs the ditch above their house, she will think of the grooves alongside the lane where a bad toss lands your ball.

Father Finch will think pinball.

·

Charlie's sister thinks pinball is stupid. It is all pretty stupid, the stuff her brother likes. Her dad's pretty stupid, too. She doesn't like his ties much. She hates the way he glares at her over his Ask Me glasses, the bridge nudged to the kink in his nose. That's his teacher face. He is going to rout her out. *For-*

the-thousandth-time—it's that face. He puts it on, for instance, when she mixes up crowbar and rebar, or concrete and cement.

•

Concrete is when the stuff hardens. Cement, you can pour and move.

Cement is what a debris flow looks like, or—if you are Charlie Finch's sister—maybe pudding. Pudding with raisins being turned with a spoon but the raisins are VDubs and flowerpots, twisted deer and laptops, Barbie dolls and shoes. They are boulders the size of pickup trucks, and Ricky Booth's daddy's pickup truck, and Ricky Booth still inside—a kid her brother's age, belted in, in his ball cap still, just smothered.

It's a wave; it's a wall in motion.

The flow sounds like a plane, like an earthquake. It sounds like thunder coming. It is dirt and trees and boulders in a stew higher than the eaves of their house. There's a coyote in it, and cactus. There are picks and forks and shovels.

•

It shoves right in through the door. The kitchen Mother Finch has carefully swept is torn up in the space of a minute, brimming with the rising crud. She sees a deer in it, still thrashing, and the dull bent bodies of horny toads and her Charlie's hightop shoes. The windows pop loose and the front door is off and the freezer is on the move. She's got to move. She is screaming, maybe—she can't remember. She remembers slogging through the stuff and dragging herself to the stairs. "The flood was coming up behind me," she remembers, "as fast as I could move."

She found her husband in his study with his headphones on, still typing, typing away. Her daughter was re-braiding her hair.

Debris had stuffed the lower story of the house by then. It thrust a branch up the stairwell. The branch bashed a hole into the attic and then the lights were gone.

The house was roaring. They could get to the attic, maybe—but somebody had to wake Charlie.

Charlie Finch was still asleep and dreaming, poking sticks into the pulsing holes. His face grew boggy, and flattened out like a field. Every hole in it went right on shining.

.

Shining!

Until his bunk floated up—which waked him.

.

Why she indulged him in a goddamn bunk bed, Father Finch would never know. The boy was spoiled. His mother wasn't a normal mother. She wasn't the sort of mother who sensed things, she had no instinct, no knowledge of things: *She should have known.* This would be Father Finch's line of thinking—soon, on the roof in the dark, the house roaring.

Charlie's bed floated up and pinned him against the starry ceiling of his room. He was awake but he couldn't move. "I can't move," he said to his mother.

His mother found his foot with her hands in the dark. She hauled back on it, and screamed: she had torn her Charlie's foot off, and was holding the skin in her hands.

She was on the ladder and the flow had climbed to the rivets in her jeans. It was cold. She couldn't feel much. She had stiffened up, standing in it.

She would have to try the other foot, the foot that was still on. She had thrown the skin down—it was a sock, you might have guessed. You might have guessed that a woman as weak as Mother Finch could not tear her boy apart with her hands.

Her Charlie was bigger than she was. She was small for her age; she always had been.

She found a foot in the dark and hauled back on it. Nothing budged. She thought to wedge in beside her boy, to lie with him, as she used to do, but he took up all the room in the bed.

Mother Finch couldn't find Charlie's foot again and when she found it again she hauled back on it and her husband was shouting from the attic, she guessed, and then he seemed to be in the room.

He seemed to be up there with her, thank God: He would know what to do. She heard him pop the lid on the skylight, and felt the rain come through.

Then he was through it, he was on the roof. He had thought it all sensibly through. He hauled his wife up onto the roof by her hair and from there they got hold of Charlie's feet and hauled back at once and he moved.

He is a powerful man, Charlie Finch's father. His boy weighed maybe ninety pounds.

Charlie slept on his back. He had been a breech birth. From the first, they had almost lost him.

Charlie was in his bed all wrong, considering. They couldn't get to his head to help him. They had to bend him a way a body won't bend at the joint unless you break it. They hauled back on him. They got his feet out in the rain. Something yielded. The knees were snapped. They kept at it. "Now," said his father.

Their boy moaned. Their daughter shouted their names from the attic, braiding and unbraiding her hair. They hauled back on him.

His mother said, soothingly, "Charlie."

Charlie wanted her to keep on saying it.

He had had a grandfather named Tecumseh, but Charlie was the name for him.

"Charlie, Charlie," his mother said.

Something cold was on him. It was pushing against his face. He couldn't get up and walk on his face any more. He couldn't skate down the hill to school.

He was cold. He had holes in his face—that wouldn't matter to her.

His mother would bring him a blanket.

Hold your horses, love. She smelled of roses.

Charlie, Charlie Finch, he thought. Little Charlie Finch, he thought.

Who was afraid to die. And then he did.

the last doll never opens

The one brother slept in the front room for going on ninety years.

This was Harold. Who once leaned into a girl in the blowing woods and lifted her skirt and kissed her.

Once the brothers lived with their sister, now dead. She wore her hair in two braids. She liked pudding, and the idea she had of the sea. She died away first while the lilacs bloomed, among the bounty of last year's honey.

Still the brothers lived on in the brick house their mother and father had hauled up from downcountry. Hauled it brick by brick by mule. One mule lived to be fifty; Harold said good night to her each night.

Good night, Cordelia, deaf and crippled, tender button, you old ruin.

•

Thanks to Cordelia, it was, Harold could see. He had rolled the Farmall in the ripened grass, dreaming of the girl he had kissed. Struck his head against a stone and was blind, not but a boy.

He was a man when, at last, the mule swung around and, where he had struck his head years before, kicked him. All it took— who would have thought?—and Harold saw again.

Saw his hand first thing and it surprised him, how soft and plump and pale.

The bees had been Harold's work all the years he was blind but his knees came unstrung once he saw them.

He never did see that girl again. She was pretty enough, only grown.

•

Harold drew into himself like a beetle, his brother said.

"He walked out of his body and died."

Born and died in the bed in the front room, same bed, their mother's boy. Now only the last one was left.

Their rooster began to come at him every time he turned his back. Their bees swarmed.

A parrot appeared in the chicken coop, ragged and half alive, and Clarence built it a perch in the kitchen. There it squawked for his sister, forty years dead, every time he chipped a dish.

A woodpecker pecked at his window at night. An owl stood in the oak and died there, died standing, its talons sunk into the branch.

•

Clarence could sit in his brother's chair, at least, and feel the last of its satin expanses.

He wasn't lonely so much as tired. He watched the birds give up on the bird feeder it had been Harold's work to fill. A few came and went. The librarian came and the town clerk, bringing milk and butter and cookies, enough for a growing family, isn't that the way.

Harold was dead but he didn't seem to be.

•

He seemed elsewhere. Shearing sheep. He must be kneeling in the barn in the filthy wool, the animal stricken and calm. He was brush hogging, or fixing fence. Reading a rule from his cookbook, nodding off in the front room.

Now at last I can sleep in that front room where I have wanted to all these years, Clarence thought. *The dog asleep on my feet; my feet are cold.*

The dog was Lucky.

Clarence had never once kissed a girl.

Clarence, Harold, Constance, the parrot called, in a voice Clarence remembered of his mother. It called the name he remembered of the girl Harold kissed.

The owl stood in the tree, faced away from the house, exactly like something living.

•

He had better sleep and hop to it come morning. Dig potatoes. Pickle beans. Sweep the cellar.

He had better try his hand trimming poor Cordelia's toes, turned up like elfin slippers.

It was Harold's work but Clarence would do it. He would heap up manure so the ground wouldn't freeze so he could bury the mule, unless she lasted. Butcher the hog. Before the cold too much.

He didn't want to but he would do it. He would tend to the bees, slow in the cold, each with a stone on its back.

·

Good night, Clarence, he thought to say. *Good night, Lucky.*

He drew the blanket back. The bed smelled of his brother. The dog would sleep on his feet.

Hallelujah.

pemmican

Verona was a woman whose tombstone would read: *I Asked Little.*

•

She had a boy named Little Five Points and Little Five Points wanted a mouse.

The rig cost her sixty-three dollars. Sawdust. Wheel. Glass house. Food. Little Five Points wanted all of it.

His first mouse, he named Verona. All night of both long nights she lived, Verona sprinted without the least complaint on her squeaking wheel. She was a plain mouse and seemed to know it. Little Five Points made a brown house for her with a curtain of pleasing beads. They passed the hours happily, small boy, plain mouse, until the third night, when death took her. Nobody up to now knows why.

•

Next came Basket and Macaroni, nothing but trouble with these two. These were fancy pants and iconoclasts, spotted from tip to toe. The clerk handed them off in a paper sack. He had a mirror glued to the top of his shoe to look up ladies' skirts with. "Hurry home," he suggested, and they did.

This goes badly. Fast. They are driving. Little Five Points holds his paper sack dutifully between his knees. The stinkers eat through the sack. They make off with his stiffened French fry and his pemmican and his goo. They live a life of furry princes in the tunnels and vents of Verona's car and trot up her skirts while she drives.

.

She drives into a moose, *numero uno.*

Numero dos: she drives into a drunken bear.

.

Verona buys three more mice for her boy. She thinks maybe the problem is numbers. She carries them home in their glass house. Surprise. Little Five Points picks out the prettiest to pet. The mouse nips him and Little Five Points whacks it against the wall. It dies instantly, what a relief.

.

He never does name the others: they fall to eating each other before he names them and Verona walks what-is-left-of-them into the snow by their wrinkling tails.

.

It could be worse, Verona reminds herself. They could be thriving in her car with Basket and that patchy Macaroni, eating the stiffened French fries Little Five Points forgets from his box.

•

She sets traps for them. Sympathetic traps with a dollop of peanut butter inside. The car smells of pee and poopy dots. The trap doors swing shut but she finds nothing, not even a smidgen of peanut butter, not even a slick where the dollop sat.

•

Poor Verona. Little Five Points wants more mice. Verona has lied to him about all of them, about Verona and the nameless cannibals and almost catching Basket. "They got out," Verona tells him. "They went to live with the hair and the corn cobs and their little wild sisters in the walls."

•

Little Five Points wants an ant farm. He wants to watch red ants steal the black ants' babies and make the black babies slaves.

Little Five Points wants a boa constrictor. He wants a baby reindeer. Little Five Points wants a Gila monster. Verona says, Whoa.

Boa constrictor, Verona thinks. Maybe she can rent one? *Scenario numero tres.*

•

Verona rents a cat from the shelter and turns it loose in her car. The cat howls all night and shreds the seats and snags its teeth in her forehead before bounding off through the snow. She comes into the kitchen bloodied. Little Five Points is spelling his name out with ketchup in his scrambled eggs. He says, "F-I-V-E. Something red is on you."

•

Verona packs them off to work, to school. She tries to reason with the mice while driving: the bitterness of winter nights, Little Five Point's happiness, the yellow wheel, etc. The mice sit on the cushy headrest, enlivened by heat and conversation, nibbling at their fries.

•

She can't bring herself to drive, *scenario numero cuatro*. She's afraid to even step near her car. She gets fired from her job for not doing it. The bank repos their house. They have to live in her car. The mice gnaw them to the bone, etc. and plump their nests with Little Five Point's lovely spun-gold hair.

•

Numero cinco. She quits driving: the mice need heat from the engine to live. Ha. The stinkers freeze solid as wood frogs. Verona burns up seven tanks of gas, elated, spring at last, blasting heat through the defrost vent until the mice are crunchy as peanuts.

•

Seis. The fuckers prosper. Multiply. The babies spit out babies in the space of a week, Mother of God, think of that, translucent pink collapsible sacks that clog the tubes, the tailpipe, an exponential increase, victors of the universe, Verona's car a mouse farm, should have made it Lucite, it's hopeless to resist them, savvy and hard at it like on the ant farms Little Five Points admires so in school.

•

Little Five Point's papa comes back to them and kisses Verona on her seeping wound and loves her slow until sunup and brings her scrambled eggs in bed. He doesn't know what he was thinking to think he could live without her. He doesn't exist without her. Tell me what you want, my life. *Scenario numero siete.*

•

"Mata! Mata!" Verona shrieks, swinging her arms and dreaming. They'll haul her off if she's not careful. She finds poopy dots in her toothbrush, poopy dots in her hair. Mice are all over her dreams. "Mata! Mata!"

•

Verona is no natural mother. The mice are one way she knows.

•

She tries a neck-snapping trap Little Five Points finds. He finds his mouse in her trap. She is never ever forgiven. He runs away at the age of six and passes his days in hiding in some ghastly European country: *scenario numero ocho.*

•

This has gone on much too long. Verona resorts to poison. They'll blow up slow with their tongues hung out. Ha, she thinks. But she can't do it. Verona thinks of the handsome Indian man who gave a talk in the town park once who said the white man ought to ask of the animal, "What do you know?" He told a story of a mouse who saved a small boy from a buffalo stampede. Of dogs who sniff out your heart attack and whimper when your insulin spikes.

•

Verona shuts the door. The mice are convened on the dashboard in the numinous green of the speedometer light.

"What do you know?" Verona asks them.

"You have seven lives," Macaroni tells her, "and you already used up six."

"Your ex will never come back to you," Basket says. "Little Five Points will join the army and marry a dowdy Kraut."

"To get away from you, the little shit."

"She will plump him up and his hair will fall out and he will never remember your birthday, not one stinking time."

"Not one?" Verona wonders.

"She'll ruin everything."

"She'll vote for the wrong president. She'll sigh and roll her eyes."

Verona picks at a scab.

"A real hatchet," Basket says. "She'll hate children."

"She already hates them now."

"She knocks them on their heads off the monkey bars."

"She yanks downs their skirts in the lunch room when their trays are heaped with food."

Verona jerks her scab free and winces.

"Can we have that?" Basket says.

"Tell me one thing more."

"Deal," say the mice, excited. Their whiskers quiver. Their mouths are wet.

"Soon, you will write a story about us. You will hit a deer on a bicycle, thinking of how to be funny. Skip it, is our advice.

You will be a teeninsy bit funny, but only when you think to say poopy dot."

"Poopy dot," Verona says.

"Very funny," say the mice, and squeeze two neat seeds onto the dashboard.

•

Verona writes a story about a race of mice who grow themselves from seed, a tiny whole mouse in every stool they put out. The white mice steal the black mouse babies and train them to clean up carefully the wreck the white mice make of the world. They are friendly and obedient. They eat plutonium and plastic. That raft of garbage bigger than Texas that is floating around in the ocean? The mice nibble through that in days.

•

It is a children's book and grownups love it. The book sells wildly. Verona is stinking rich. She gives every nickel away.

•

She runs an ad for a Handsome Indian who replies pronto and falls in love with her. He makes a terrific daddy. Little Five Points learns to catch after all. He wrestles and grunts in the green grass and ties his shoes before school.

This can't last. Verona is on her last life: Basket and Macaroni were right. She picks a good day to die and dies happy, a saint almost, radiant and deranged, recalling the masses she raised up from nothing to make this a better world.

milk river

Their fathers had taken to calling them *Mother*.

They had brothers in the war; mothers dead. They had lockets of hair in their lockers at school; trouble at school; chores.

They filled pillow-sacks with pole beans. The girls milked and pickled and doctored and cooked and kept the hotrod running they were too young yet to drive. Still, they drove it, nights, on the county roads, the headlights off, throwing back a veil of dust.

They would marry men from faraway places.

They would find where Crazy Horse lay. The white man came like water then—Blixruds and Wenderoths, Crarys and Dahls and Otters. Coming, coming, coming. Yellow dust in the Black Hills. Red Cloud, He Dog. Looking Glass and Sitting Bull. The girls had studied them all in school.

"You're a pretty smart cookie, for a cookie," Franny said.

Hoka hey, she said. *Wasichu.*

•

In the dusk of the month of the sinking grass, the girls lay in the fields where the wheat grew. They dribbled dirt on each other's faces. The dirt was silver, amended, a chemical ash.

The night was warm. The fields were shorn. Chickadees fattened upon them. The girls lay on their backs against the stubble of wheat, the sheared-off hollow pegs, dispersing their weight as they had been schooled to do when caught on ice that is breaking.

Crazy Horse had not been crazy, they knew. He was touched. He had been laid to rest, left for the birds. Crazy Horse was near and far. His blood ran in the birds, in the antelope; it ran in the fish of the river. They had found a cloth he wore. They found his tooth in the silt of the river, one summer when the water warmed.

When the water warmed, the story goes, when their mothers carried the girls in their bellies, two fine feathers, glossy and black, came to them on the wind. Which is to say: their babies would be girls. They would keep to home when the wars began, when their brothers leaned from the windows of the car, tossed out their kisses, and waved. Good boys, gallant, each with a foot in the grave.

The boys had written for months to their mothers, who were dead. Now the boys wrote to their sisters. They sent them treasures: a broken shoelace, a dimpled stone. The cellophane wing of a locust. For every boy in their town who had fallen, they sent a pinch of dust. *Be good to Poppy,* they wrote. *Feed the dogs.*

The dogs, too, had fallen—the one dog mauled in the thresher, another gone by in sleep. The girls' brothers knew nothing of this; the girls kept the news to themselves. For months, they kept the news of their mothers from the boys: they sent only news of the living, the newly living, the pups and calves and foals.

They kept—in a coffee can—in a time capsule—every last little thing their brothers sent them. They kept the key to the hotrod there, and a scrap of hair or feather or hide of anything slaughtered or fallen. They kept pictures of girls—goofy mall shots—their brothers had kissed and sworn themselves to.

If they married, these girls, or rode out to the buttes with boys too young to enlist, too crippled or scared, the sisters would burn their pictures. They would push tacks into the faces of dolls they had named for their brothers' sweethearts, and bury the dolls in the barn.

•

Their mothers had died days away from one another, days the cold made jewels of the snow. Their mothers had been girls together. They dressed up in the ruffled dresses of the pioneer women before them and rode their ponies sidesaddle through the door of the one-room school. They roped gophers, and shot them through with arrows, and sawed off their tails as an offering to the chiefs they mostly loved. They loved the peaceable chiefs and the savage, the deliriums they could dizzy to when they spun in the remnant tepee rings on the bluffs above the milky river. They gave thanks in the four directions, from which the white horse and the dappled surged, the red horse of the springtime rains, the black of the east loping six-by-six over the darkening plain. They were girls. They would come to be wives together—too soon. Too late to marry Looking Glass. Too late to marry Mort Clark, wavy-haired golden boy, blasted out of a cloudless sky in the last world war.

"I'm him," Franny said, "I'm Mort Clark—" her mother's love, high school days, a golden boy; she'd seen pictures. Franny rolled across the stubble of wheat and kissed Magdalena without knowing she would on her open mouth.

"You poor, poor boy," said Magdalena.

"Franny," Franny said, and her throat burned.

She was Mort Clark speaking to her mother. She was a girl in a field in autumn. She said, "Nothing ever happened to me. Nothing ever will."

•

Franny had been her mother's name. There were Blixruds all through that dry country.

Hoka hey was a greeting.

Wasichu was a name for the buffalo when buffalo were everywhere and next a Sioux name for the white man when like water he came and came.

It went wheat and wheat and canola now, advancing on the backbone of the Rockies. To the east: the white bluffs where Crazy Horse lay. Their mothers lay beyond that, in the burying ground above the river, with their heads to the rising sun.

The mothers tapped at their daughters' windows still. *Have you written to your brothers?* they wanted to know.

Blanched the beans? Don't forget. Mulch the rose.

The cold, after all, was coming. The girls ought to shove bales of straw against the skirts of their houses now, before the wind grew teeth, before the snow blew. Already the trees were picked clean. The scrub had turned the russet of potatoes.

•

Their fathers had taken to calling them *Mother*, they had taken to their chairs. They slept sitting, holding their heads in their hands. The skin of their hands was dappled, lovely as the bark of the sycamore, as a field of wheat in sun the wind moves the clouds out over.

The swans, too, were moving; the geese were going, gone. The girls lay in the dark beneath them. They pulled their shirts off.

"I dreamed," Maggie said, "of an ocean, and the whales rose up from below me, and rolled me across their backs."

Their mothers lived still. Which is to say: the girls felt them drawing near. Their mothers stood in the fields and watched them.

Live, little chicken, they said, *live.*

Their mothers sang in the lee of the shelterbelt in the wind that bristled through the caragana.

Skippy the giant, they reminded, *keep away from him. I saw him steal a dollar from his mother once. He crushed a hummingbird, remember, in his hands.*

Their fathers slept with their heads in their hands. They wintered over. They had wintered over since earliest green, through tilling and planting and harvest. They slept in their chairs with their boots on. By God, they would die with their boots on, as their people had before them. Their people had come to this country in wagons, dragging a rope to keep to a straight path across the unbroken plain. Hearty stock, pioneers, blood in every step they were taking.

They made good, proved up. Came to this.

To this!

•

The girls dribbled dirt on each other's faces, dirt on each other's necks. A marsh hawk glided above them, drawn to the flapping of a sleeve. The wind lifted their hair and dropped it. The hawk swooped, seized something small, a vole, a shrew, carried it off in its talons. It was a sign, but the girls did not know of what.

They knew snow would shore up in the shelterbelt, in the caragana and the olive trees, the whistling Lombardi poplar. Shutaway days; a gnawing wind.

A day would come the wind would quit and cold would make jewels of the snow. That would be the day, come around again, that Franny's mother had walked to the river, climbed the wide dappled sycamore tree, and on the rope her boy had swung from, summers when the water was warm, let herself down to die.

Let me die, she prayed, *before him.*

•

The girls pulled apart their old Barbies and hung their heads in the trees. They painted each other's toenails. They took turns with each other's hair.

"Do you want to look like you, or me?" they asked.

They looked like sisters. They could look, with effort, like twins, as their mothers had before them. They could dream the same dream, they swore it.

They turned cartwheels. They walked on their hands underwater, months when the water was warm.

They knew birdsongs: *chickadee dee dee. Who cooks, who cooks, who cooks for you?* They knew one hawk from another, and how a marsh hawk's head, in flight, tips down.

They knew Sitting Bull was murdered. Crazy Horse was murdered. He was Curly, the years he was young.

Would that they had lived when Crazy Horse lived! They would have been a sweetness to him, little fierce Ogallala wives.

·

Dark settled on the plain and, with it, the nightly thimble of dew. Franny's goat appeared—she was a milk goat—she had been Franny's brother's goat—her teats were leaking. Her brother used to lie down under the goat and squirt milk onto his tongue.

Now the goat went where Franny went, as with the little lamb of the song. It stood above the girls in the wheat field.

"She needs milking."

"I'd say."

"Poppy's hungry," Franny said, "he must be. What if he's bumping around in the barn?"

"He'll dream that horsy dream again. And then he'll thrash you."

So they stayed. Or: and yet they stayed.

They dribbled dirt on each other's bellies, spelling out the names they were given. They spelled out the names of the animals they had lost since their brothers went to war—Bonky and Marmalade, the old tom Hopsalot.

The mother cat, they lost to the weasel—easy pickings. The weasel was fearless, the girls knew, a great hunter, a great mouser. It killed for fun.

Their brothers killed because they had to—like their fathers, and the fathers before them. Except they liked it. The girls could swear their brothers liked it—the hat, at least, and buttons, the snappy, glistening shoes. They couldn't stop swiping dust from their shoes.

Never mind that the town nearly shut down to watch them rocket off in the hotrod. Forget the women, their swallowed pitiful tremolo; forget the goofy bump of a hug their Poppies tried to give them, to see them off, *g'luck, son:* the boys were swiping at their goddamn shoes.

Shoes in a shine you saw yourself in.

When you were a little boy, their mothers kept saying, until something in the saying snagged them, sent them off into the barn among the horses to sob until another mother brought them back.

It's hard, honey. But you've got to.

And the kids, the littler ones, whipped each other with Twizzlers; and the men drank Pabst from sweating cans; and the goat stood up on the table and drank from the good glass punch bowl.

The day lasted—hot and blue. The horses whinnied in the barn. A mother set out a sprinkler the littler kids bumbled through. August, and the hoppers had come, and the wheat was ripe in the fields.

At last, the boys set out. Saying, *Love you, Mother. Quit now. Mother, mind the goddamn shoes.*

•

You couldn't predict it: the weasel would kill every chicken in the chicken coop. Partridge, it killed, once a coyote. It killed the mother cat and left the kittens alive for the girls to save and mother.

The kittens were toothless still and tiny, weepy eyed; their ribs showed. The girls fed them out of an eyedropper—milk warm from the goat, from the cow.

Maggie rolled onto a kitten and crushed it where it had crept into her bed. The hens blinded another. Franny carried the rest in the sling of her shirt until the close of school.

The girls walked home together, bumping hips, the kittens mewling. "Show you something," Franny said.

They stood in Franny's kitchen. Franny dipped her fingers in a pitcher of milk and bunched Maggie's shirt beneath her chin. Franny's head swam. Her mouth went dry.

She went by feel, not watching, and dabbed the milk at Maggie's breast. She held a kitten to her, let it root and mew. Their breasts had puffed up—just enough, and the buds were like satin, and the kittens latched softly on.

·

Their mothers had been girls together; the girls were little mothers together. Their clothes smelled of the barn, of the animals fed, of the milk goat freshly feasted on whatever trash it could find. The goat followed the girls to school one day and stood in the playground bleating.

Hicks, they were called, and *lesbo cows. You stink of cow. Bet she stuck her arm in a cow before school. Yeah, yeah, yeah. And the other lesbo licked it.*

The girls kept to themselves at school.

They kept a box of crickets in their lockers at school to remind them of the time that would have to pass before they would meet again. They dropped a cricket in a shoe or a pocket, to sing the little song it harbored—the weakening *hurry hurry* it sang, slow in the cold, in the sinking grass, sounding the song of its kin.

"How long is the life of a cricket?" they asked.

"Not very, not very, not very."

•

The marsh hawk came back.

A star burned out.

Maggie heard it; the star hissed as it fell; it whimpered. No: "That's the goat, silly—" Franny's milk goat was squatting in the dirt to pee.

The goat had lived twice as long as it should have, eating snuff and the hoppers of August.

The goat stamped its feet. It wheezed at the girls.

"We should go."

"I should write to Billy."

"The chickens need fed."

Still they lay there. "Go away, go away."

"Go to Bismarck?"

"Go home."

"He'll thrash me with that stupid rodeo belt he won when he was a boy," Franny said.

"Your poppy was never a boy," Maggie said.

"Boys," Franny said. "Good God."

·

The goat followed them, butting them, home.

It was the tinging of the bell around the neck of the goat that waked Franny's father from his dream. He was dreaming his dream of horses, the one from when he was a boy. Except now the dream happens in a corn palace; now when the horse comes at him, he has a whole corn room to move.

Except he can't: his boots are filled with quarters.

He was a boy on a dare, a greenhorn creeping into a stall. Only boy, a mother's prize—a boy whose claim to courage was the mangling, once, of frogs. He was terrified of horses. He was terrified of frogs.

He crept in from the sun and the stall was dark. The other boy, a neighbor boy, slid the lock to and watched him over the wooden door.

The horse came at him. It wheeled, reared, struck him. It had a blaze of white that veered wildly over its whitened eye.

This, some half-a-dozen decades ago.

Still, night upon night he waked shouting, not knowing where he was. He was alone, he remembered, crippled up, an old man dropped into sleep in his boots in a dead dry country.

He rose, shuffled into the kitchen. It was night yet, he saw, for the stars were out, the moon was smoothly passing.

He called out, "Franny."

He was a boy, else a dog, or a man, newly loved. He was not himself, waked from a dream, seeing his daughter in the lemony kitchen. He saw instead his wife—a girl. *Franny, Franny.* There she was.

She was turned from him, her rope of hair. She smelled of the dirt of the fields, the shit of cattle and horses.

She would wait for him. She would come to be his wife. After the war, years ago, she would come to be his wife. She would wait for the war to be over, as she had, as she would, then as now.

She was turned from him, at her chores.

"Whosoever shall," he mumbled, "whosoever shall—" but he had lost the words that follow.

He went to her, and stood behind her with his hands on her belly. Franny's father had the hands of a milker. His fingers curled; he couldn't straighten them; his palms were slabs, mottled and raw.

He bunched her shirt up, lay his mouth against her neck. Franny twisted away and he followed her as a dog would, or a goat. When she stopped—to dry the dishes, to stir the soup—he came behind her, shuffling in his split-apart boots, and leaned against her back.

A good girl, strong—she would look after him.

"Go rest, Poppy. Lie down."

He never lay down, night or day any more. He slept where he could see, should he sleep, holding his head in his hands. He saw the yard, the barn, the path his daughter walked to school. He saw the girls bump at the hip when they walked, as their mothers had before them. They sang in the dark of the hay mow, where the light pressed, in bolts of gold, between the boards of the barn.

They made a joyful noise—singing songs their mothers had sung, in their mothers' plain, thin voices.

It was a trick: you couldn't tell between them. They were elated; they might be grieving. They might be one voice, or four.

His head was roaring; he couldn't hear her now. He couldn't see into the barn.

If only she would let him see her!

One last time, he thought. His wife was singing. He would go to her. He tried to stand up. The dog was lying on his feet.

What was the matter with him? Hadn't he seen her, a day the sun burned on the snow, lowered into the grave?

Yet he lived. This was his house yet, his chair. His yet: the sun in the trees, the sinking grass. He had wintered over. He was dying, this much was clear. Yet he lived—an old man in a dead dry country. Widow man, cripple.

He pressed the great slabs of his hands hard against his ears, not to hear her.

He stood in the doorway, so to hear her.

His wife was singing him over to her, hesitating on the great divide.

•

Franny's brother from the war sent her a shoe worn by a child he had shot (a mistake), a seepage of dust from the desert. Into the toe of the shoe, he had folded this note: *Dear little sister lollipop, you will not see me alive again.*

Franny wrote: Poppy sleeps with his boots on. He does not want to die in his socks.

He doesn't talk much, but he remembers to go out and milk the cow eleven times a day. He thinks I am Mother or, some days, a girl he has never seen.

How old was the girl you sent the shoe of to me? What color was her hair?

I put the shoe in the time capsule.

The dogs are fine. The kittens' eyes are open. I learned a new card trick to show you.

Remember the time in the schoolyard when Mother ran with you with your kite you made on a day of no wind until night fell? I found the kite in Poppy's closet behind his high-shine shoes. He wears the same boots every day. The soles have come free and they flap when he walks. His sleeves are too long. He is shrinking. Holes are burned through his shirts from smoking.

He will flame up soon, he says so, and blow the hell away.

.

She wrote: I found him lying in the kitchen with a bread sack stuffed up against his face. He had the gas line unhooked that goes to the stove and he had poked the end into the bread sack. It was a colored sack, for Rainbow bread. Sun came yellow through the frost on the window. It was pretty. It was a good day to die, I was thinking. I shouted for him to move. His shirt was off.

I am sorry to tell you this, Brother. I was only just home from school. Our poppy was lying on the floor in the kitchen. I shouted at him. If I touched him, he would sit up and bite me. It wasn't so but I thought so.

I couldn't touch him but then I did. I thought how I carried the dog that died and the stillborn calf and the foal. I thought of the Sioux at Wounded Knee carrying off their dead, and of the baby Black Elk tells us was nursing from its dead mother. I thought of Mother in her tree we swung from.

You have got to please come home.

I pulled the sack off. His skin was warm from the sun. I carried him out to his chair. I could carry him! Poppy is tiny.

I went, *pops poppy lollipop, little sister lollipop,* talking to myself.

His skin is spattered with scars from the embers that fall and burn through his shirts when he smokes. He snatches at the air when he sleeps.

Maggie and I like to watch him sleep. He looks like a boy catching fireflies like in August when you were here.

Oh, but, Brother, I need to tell you. They got him rushed down in the ambulance, Brother, and Dr. Gene brought him back. So he is back now. They brought him back without his boots on, which I tore up the house to look for. He goes barefoot like an Indian now. His toenails are curved and yellow and the shit from when he milks the cow is stuffed in underneath them. *Bring me this,* he says, *bring me that, I can't move for the dog lying on me.*

But he can still milk the cow, I told you, elevendy-leven times a day.

·

Please you should write to me, Brother, and let me know that you are fine. It is a long time now since word came. The leaves are all down and the snow blows in. The wind gnaws at the house, you remember.

She wrote: Maggie hardly comes to the house any more. She is too afraid of Poppy.

I have started skipping school. Poppy wants me here every day now to iron his good shirts. He wants to look nice for the street dance that comes before the rodeo you remember on the Fourth of July.

Remember the once that bull rider got flipped over the fence into Mother? Poppy remembers. He remembers the float like a pirate ship and the veterans in a cage of barbed wire with their banner that says *Thank me*. It has been the Fourth of July for a month now.

Even so, even with me home ironing, Poppy wants to iron, too. Today he left the iron flat on his shirt until it was black and smoking. He irons Mother's clothes I never moved from their place. He holds the iron to the bottoms of her shoes. *This will keep her,* he says, *from walking.*

He says he will do it to me, too. *You better quit,* he says.

I need you, he says. *Don't you ever go away.*

•

Still I go at least to Maggie's, when the snow is soft to be quiet. It has snowed every night for a week now so in the morning my tracks are gone. I go to Maggie's and we listen to music very low and she lets me brush her hair. She gives me all the peanuts from her Cracker Jacks.

We ride out in the hotrod with the lights shut off to the bluffs where the tepee rings are. The rings are gone underneath the snow but we know if we are standing in them. We spin until we fall down and the stars smear wild and blue. The crows are black on the snow. The town sleeps at our feet. I pretend that I am Crazy Horse and Maggie is my pretty young squaw.

•

Remember we went to Montana that time and all the little trails the Indians made to where Looking Glass fell and the women in the swale dug themselves in with their hands? It was hot and Mother made us walk. The wind came up, it was a hot wind, and we didn't want to walk. And we saw a deer in the rushes.

We knew the speech Chief Joseph spoke when they had come so near to the Medicine Line after months of flight and fighting and no help came down from Sitting Bull because the messengers were killed. Mother knew the speech, too, and we said it: *Hear me, my chiefs. I am tired. My heart is sick and sad.*

Remember? *Looking Glass is dead. Too-hul-hul-sote is dead. The old men are all dead. It is the young men who say yes or no. Hear me, my chiefs.*

I can't remember all of it. *It is cold and we have no blankets.*

We stood at the stone with our hands high and the sun burned down on our faces. I felt the wind lift my hair; it was a hot wind. It moved your shirttails. You stood between us.

And we said, *It is cold and we have no blankets. The little children are freezing to death. My people, some of them, have run away to the hills. No one knows where they are—perhaps freezing to death. I want to have time to look for my children and see how many of them I can find.*

You were between us. We turned away from the sun. And you said, "Yeah, but I'm still going."

We watched that dirty poodle, remember, squeeze out a stool at the foot of the stones that stood in the sun where Chief Joseph stood?

Mother kicked at the poodle. And you said, "Yeah, but I'm still going."

And that night all night in Minot, Mother sat in the tub in the hotel and we listened to her cry and cry.

·

And now you are gone and no word comes and Mother hanged herself in the tree. And now I cannot go to Maggie's.

Poppy is like a dog. The snow came on to hide my tracks and I went in the night and quiet and it was quiet yet when I came home and Poppy was in his chair. I slept and, when I waked, the sun was up and he was standing over me. He had the iron in his hands.

How he knew is we never have Cracker Jacks and he could smell them on my hands, he said, and he said my breath stank of them.

Poppy sat on my feet and the iron was hot and he touched it to my heel. He touched first the one next the other.

Now he won't let me go to school. We are here in this house just the two of us and the snow has come and come. Still he thinks there will be the street dance. He will go there and dance with Mother.

He has hung a good snap shirt with a bolo tie on every chair in the house now. His high-shine shoes—every one of them is out there in the snow.

When I go to the barn, I hopscotch not to step in the shoes he used to wear that serve to mark the path now between the house and the barn. She is sleeping in the barn with the horses, he thinks.

He will catch her there one day soon.

·

One day a stack of letters tied with a string will arrive for me from you. It will be a day like the movies. Let it please come soon.

•

She wrote: Is it true where you are that water appears and you walk and it goes away? I would like to see that.

I would like to see a place where no roads go and wind takes your footprints away. The hills move in the wind. They are nothing but sand. Nothing holds them. I would like to see what grows there. I would like to see what lives.

I see no one but the animals and Poppy, and Poppy's shirts and shoes, and Poppy's trail he has worn going barefoot to milk the cow in the barn. His feet are cracked and bleeding. I rub salve on them that is for the horses' hooves but they are foul to smell or look at.

Poppy could walk on coals, he thinks.

My feet are too awful soft, he thinks. He says, The river of fire on the great divide—how will I ever cross it?

"I will have to cross it with you," he says. "I will carry you on my head."

He crosses to the barn and comes back with a dribble of milk in his bucket and his feet are red and raw.

"Don't they hurt you?" I ask him.

He can't feel them. He only feels that the dog lies on them, he says, so he says, "Bring me this, bring me that."

But, Brother, I am sorry to tell you. That dog is dead going on a year now and buried behind the barn.

Poppy's shoes disappear in the snow every night. He shakes out the snow in the morning and sets them back on the path for Mother. He says Mother has her nose to go by, too, by the bloody seep his feet leave fresh in the sun in the fresh fall between the house and the barn.

He hears her singing in the barn, he says. But when he comes near, she is quiet.

He says, "When I was a boy we went quiet to the pond in our socks so the frogs wouldn't quit. But they quit," he says, "they always."

•

You ought to quit, too, and come home, Brother. You are hiding in your shiny shoes, Poppy says. He says you should never have gone.

He says, "*Widow*, we say, and *widower*. But what is the name for the mother of the boy who gets himself killed in a war? What is the name for the father?"

God willing, you will come back home. You will ride in your hat with the high-shine bill with the pissy old men from the rest of the wars, and the widows will throw you roses, and you will think always: *Thank me.*

I would thank you always, Brother. I would thank you to come straight home.

•

We hear that Earl is dead and Dr. Gene's boy and Looks At The Stars from the rez. Carol Ann came home from the corner store who can neither speak nor hear. She sits in a big chair shaking.

Maggie's brother is killed, we have heard it. I am here and cannot go to her, but I know the word has come.

She wears her hair over her face now. Her poppy makes her go to school. She still walks by our house and waves, Brother, on her way to school. She left a cricket for me from under her bed and a note that said your Suzie. Your Suzie is going with an eastern boy, so I pushed tacks into the doll of her and buried her in the barn.

This is the news I know of, Brother. Poppy says you can't hide from it all.

You can run, he says, but it always.

Poppy says you put a noose around Mother's neck and ran away off to the war.

•

Poppy pounds against the windows. He shakes his fists at the trees. He is like something in a cage with the door standing wide with the cold and the snow streaming in.

Send word.

She wrote: I would like to see sun so hot and soft it looks to melt out of the sky. Camels, I would like to see, with rubies hanging down from their halters. The camels kneel in the sand. The sky is burning. The sand is the color of my skin that you sent, so hot you cannot walk across it.

•

Poppy sits on my feet in the night, Brother. He is small but I cannot get him off me.

He hums a song our mother sang to us when I was asleep or pretended to be and she carried me over the field.

By God, he says, I got you.

He touches the iron to my heel. I cannot get him off me.

I try to slap at him. Poppy smells of the barn. I scratch at him.
It is like scratching at a fencepost, Brother.

But for the dog that lies on our poppy's feet, he cannot feel a
damn thing, he said so, from the brisket down.

·

She wrote: I would like to see Mother at my age sitting in a tree
with Mort Clark with her bare legs hanging down. They let
their legs swing. It is summer. He has painted her toenails red.
The river is slow and milky and the branch our mother sits on
makes a shadow across the water. The shadow grows long and
longer until it darkens the other side.

·

She wrote: I made my way out to Maggie's.

The sky looked like snow but it never did snow so easy you saw
my tracks going out and coming back again. We went to the
bluffs where we found the cloth, remember, that Crazy Horse
once wore? We were keeping the cloth in the time capsule with
the rest of what Maggie's brother sent and the things you sent
to us, too. We mixed the dust of the plains and the desert. We
laid a coin someone left for Looking Glass in the heel of that
little girl's shoe. We had a jewel each from each of our mothers.
A button we had not sewn on. We had the hooked toe of the
badger you shot and forgot to take to keep you and bring you
safe back home.

Maggie said, "Remember we scratched our brothers' names
in the window glass with diamond rings our mothers used to
wear? We should not have done that. We should have buried

their diamonds with them. We should have worn our brothers' clothes every day and kept a black rock in our pockets and a scrap of our brothers' hair. We sailed a feather down from the rooftop—we should not have done that. We should not have touched the hotrod our brothers set out in. And not the toothbrush. Nor the tin of snuff. Nor the gloves our brothers left in the jockey box, worn through from stacking hay. Our brothers left money in the ashtray we spent. We should have spent it on them. We spent it on ourselves."

Maggie lay down in the snow. She made me cover her over with it. I packed snow against her face how she said to until nothing showed or moved. Still she breathed and her breath, the heat of it, melted a place in the snow. And the snow came to ice that held the shape of her face and, when Maggie stood up, it was there. Her face was pressed into the snow. The ice held it.

And I thought of us, Brother, on the lake that day when we lay on the ice with Mother. The ice made a sound—*like a bear,* Mother said, *like a rocket, busting in from far away.*

We had our faces up. My braid stuck to the ice. We wore mittens. It began to snow while we lay there and we thought of the goose we saw stuck to the ice and the time the car quit in the snowstorm on the highway near to Bismarck and by morning time was buried and we didn't know was it night or day.

We lay there. You are happy, it is said, when you are freezing, and begin in the end to cross over.

The snow twisted down onto our faces, onto our coats and legs. If the ice broke, I thought, or we stuck there, only Poppy would be left to grieve. The snow came down all around us, around you and me and Mother, and we saw in the ice when we stood to leave the darker shapes in the white of the snow that showed us where we lay.

·

She wrote: Red Cloud gave up the land, it is said, when the white man found gold in the hills. You couldn't fight them. There were just too many of them, come flooding across the land.

So it is that Crazy Horse went quiet. He brooded, walking alone for days. You could walk back-to-back across the buffalo still; the great herds darkened the plains. I would like to have seen that.

Before the sheep came, and the cow, I would like, before the plow that broke the plains. Looks At The Stars. Sitting Bull. Earl. The grizzlies way out on the prairie. Neither wheat nor wagon nor wire, I would like. Before Wounded Knee and Bearcoat Miles, before the Crarys and Dahls and Otters. Before the little men from China came to lay the track over the plains, I would like. And the pioneers came. And the prospectors. And the gentlemen from St. Louis, it is said, who shot the great herds by the thousands from the windows of the passing train. For fun, they shot them.

But, Brother? Remember we had our lassoes, Brother, to lasso the passing train?

We wore clothes from flaps of leather, and we slept in the bluffs in burlap sacks with feathers in our hair. We smeared our faces red. You were Heavy Runner and, some days, the Great Goose of Doom. We raided our fields for horses. We lassoed Mother, and got her up on the yellow mare, and carried her away.

·

Crazy Horse fought and was captured, it is said. It is said that when the soldiers killed him, his people carried him off to hide.

His blood runs in the fish and the antelope, Brother, in the marsh hawk that dips its head as it flies. In the swallows lifting up without number, it runs, in the east in the brightening sky.

I am a fool, Poppy says, to believe any of this. There is no telling where Crazy Horse lies.

Poppy calls me a fool to write to you and to think you will find your way home. They have already killed you, Brother. This is what Poppy says. Poppy says they will send you back to us and we will have to burn or bury you with your head to the rising sun.

The ground will have thawed to dig then, Brother. I will help our poppy with you. Poppy says I have to. *You can run,* he says, *but it always.* They will send what they can find.